THE BEACH DATE

A SUNNY ISLE OF PALMS NOVEL (BOOK 2)

GRACE PALMER

JOIN MY MAILING LIST!

Click the link below to join my mailing list and receive updates, freebies, release announcements, and more!

JOIN HERE:

https://sendfox.com/lp/19y8p3

ALSO BY GRACE PALMER
A SUNNY ISLE OF PALMS NOVEL (BOOK 1)

Sunny Isle of Palms

The Beach Baby

The Beach Date

The Beach B&B

The Wayfarer Inn

The Vineyard Sisters

The Vineyard Mothers

The Vineyard Daughters

Sweet Island Inn

No Home Like Nantucket (Book 1)

No Beach Like Nantucket (Book 2)

No Wedding Like Nantucket (Book 3)

No Love Like Nantucket (Book 4)

No Secret Like Nantucket (Book 5)

No Forever Like Nantucket (Book 6)

Willow Beach Inn

Just South of Paradise (Book 1)

Just South of Perfect (Book 2)

Just South of Sunrise (Book 3)

Just South of Christmas (Book 4)

THE BEACH DATE

Annette Wilson doesn't know what to do.

After ten years, she's back on the Isle of Palms and reconciled with her older sister Charlene. She *thought* she'd put her old life—her cheating husband with a second family—behind her.

But she thought wrong.

Because out of nowhere, Frederick reappears on her doorstep, asking for forgiveness and a second chance.

It would be so easy—maybe *too* easy—to slip right back into the way things once were. But is that the right choice?

Or is this fresh start in her hometown—not to mention a budding connection with the handsome owner of a new local restaurant who seems to have quite an eye for Annette—what she actually needs?

Torn between the old and the new, Annette can't decide which way to turn.

Then she wakes up feeling queasy…

And her world flips upside down.

Pregnant at 40. She hardly knew such a thing was possible.

And, more to the point…

She hardly knows what to do next. Can she pick right?

1

AFTERNOON AT ANNETTE AND CHARLENE'S HOUSE—ISLE OF PALMS, SOUTH CAROLINA

Annette Campbell stood frozen in the doorway, very aware she'd nearly lost a toe.

She'd been in the middle of cutting celebratory cake slices. Her sister, Charlene, finally had the adoption papers for her grandson in hand. Tyler was going to be a permanent fixture in the house they shared. It was supposed to be a happy moment.

Then came the knock on the door.

Now, a knife covered in remnants of marshmallow frosting and chocolate ganache trembled on the entryway floor where she'd dropped it, and Annette was staring at her estranged husband.

How long had it been since she'd seen him? Ten months, right? After day 194, she'd stopped counting. Annette imagined herself flipping a *"Days Without Frederick"* tracker back to zero.

She heard the commotion behind her. Charlene wondering what was going on, Noah hot on her trail, per usual. The two of them were inseparable lately, so it made sense they'd both witness Annette going catatonic from the same vantage point.

"Annette, who is at the—?"

Charlene's voice died suddenly as Annette pushed the door open and stepped aside, showing them what she couldn't say out loud.

Frederick had on a pair of tan dockers and the button-down shirt with the tiny flowers on it that he'd worn to her college roommate Quinn's wedding. He hated it. Annette had to buy the shirt for him and then practically drag him to the affair. He'd been so grouchy throughout the entire ceremony she almost went hunting for someone else to sit by, but the open bar at the reception had softened him.

If he wanted to endear her to him, he'd chosen the wrong outfit.

Frederick's arm shot out like a spring-loaded snake from a trick can of peanuts. Annette jolted backward, surprised she hadn't noticed the twelve red roses clutched in his fist until he shoved them in her face.

What was he doing here? He had someone else to give roses to now. Actually, he'd had someone else for years. Maybe that was why he never gave Annette roses.

"They're a waste of money," he'd always gripe. *"Why would I buy something that's going to die? Not very romantic, watching a gift shrivel up on the counter, is it?"*

He probably just didn't want to buy duplicate bouquets—one for his wife, one for his mistress.

"I missed you, Annie." He shook the flowers gently.

Annette squeezed her hand into a fist. "What are you doing here?"

"I just told you: I missed you." He dropped his arm, letting the flowers dangle upside down. A petal broke away and fluttered to the ground.

"That doesn't answer the question."

"I want to talk to you."

"You should have called." Annette crossed her arms. It was high summer, but she fought back a shiver.

"You wouldn't have answered."

"Exactly," she said. "You should have called."

Frederick sighed, and Annette was immediately transported to the thousand different times she'd heard that exact same sigh.

When she suggested they visit her family for Christmas instead of tour Spain—*sigh*.

Anytime she asked him to cancel one of his bi-weekly game nights in favor of a night in with her—*sigh*.

When she took too long deciding whether to order a chicken wrap or a hamburger in the drive-thru line, or when she tried to suggest a fun date idea, or this or that or one thing or the other—*sigh, sigh, sigh*.

"It's been months, Annie. We need to talk."

"No, you need to leave. It's my nephew's birthday. There's no room for party crashers."

He frowned and tried to look past Annette into the house. "Nephew? Since when—"

Annette shifted to block the doorway. "Leave."

"I'm not leaving until we talk. This is crazy. You're my wife."

"Only in the legal sense," she said. "Our vows stopped meaning anything when you stomped all over them."

"Annie, please—"

"Leave!" Annette was glad Tyler wasn't in the foyer to hear her yell. It was his special day. She didn't want him worrying about her, sensitive little boy that he was.

Frederick opened his mouth to respond, and then stopped. His eyes shifted over Annette's shoulder.

Then Noah spoke.

"She asked you to leave." Noah wasn't especially intimidating most days, but he sure sounded scary right now. His voice was deep and seemed to rumble through the wooden boards of the porch.

"Who is this—your boyfriend?" Frederick spat, as though he had any right.

Noah moved to stand next to Annette, his arms crossed over his chest. She could see a spot of melted cheese stuck to his elbow from the mac and cheese grilled cheeses he'd made for lunch. "I'm her friend, and now I'm asking you to leave, too. Before I call the police."

"You wouldn't call the police on me." Frederick turned to Annette, his pouty face on.

"I don't think you want to stick around and test that theory," she said.

Frederick looked from Annette to Noah and back again. "Fine. I'll go. For now. But I'm not leaving town until we talk." He raised his hands —like *they* were being the crazy ones, the aggressive ones, the intrusive ones, not him—and retreated slowly down the steps.

Annette wanted to say something snarky, but she didn't have the energy. Frederick had drained it all out of her.

As soon as he turned his back, Noah slammed the door shut and Charlene pulled Annette into the entryway. Wordlessly, her sister wrapped her in a hug. Annette sunk into it gratefully.

"Has he tried to reach out before this?" Charlene slid a steaming mug of coffee across the table to Annette.

Her sister had been plying her with offers of tea and snacks and water for the last ten minutes, but Annette had refused everything. Finally, mostly just to get Charlene to settle down, she let her make her a cup of coffee.

"He has called, but I blocked his number. I didn't want to talk to him."

"For good reason," Charlene said. "What he did was... it was horrible. Unspeakable."

Noah raised a nervous hand. "Could we speak it a little bit? I'm lost."

"Oh, I'm sorry. I forgot you don't know. It's just that... well, it wasn't my story to tell. So I—I'm sorry."

"No, it's fine," he said quickly. "I don't need to know. Not if Annette doesn't want me to." He looked to Annette, a question in his eyes.

"If you're going to have to play my bodyguard every time he comes around, I think you deserve to know what's going on. The short of it is: he cheated on me. For years. And his girlfriend is pregnant." Annette gripped her mug, letting the heat nearly burn through her. "Well, I guess she has probably had the baby by now."

Her throat felt tight. Her eyes swam.

Months of forcing Frederick out of her mind—convincing herself she was free of him—undone in a single afternoon. In a single moment. In a single rose petal, fluttering to the ground.

"Now, I wish I had called the police," Noah said. "Or shoved him down the stairs, maybe. I'm sorry, Annette."

She forced a smile onto her face. "Thanks. I appreciate that."

"Of course. I'm here whenever you need me," he said.

"And I am, too. Obviously," Charlene added. "No matter what you decide."

Annette snapped her attention from the black depths of her coffee to her sister's face. "What do you mean? What decision is there to make?"

"Well, he wants to talk to you."

"So?"

"I assume that means he wants you back." Charlene shrugged, suddenly looking nervous. "That's what I'd guess, anyway."

Annette hadn't even considered that. Why hadn't she considered that? The roses. The flower shirt. Clearly, Frederick was trying to make a good impression.

"And whatever you decide, we'll be here for you. Supportive," Charlene finished.

From Annette's point of view, there was no decision to make. "I can't get back together with him."

"I mean, you can," Charlene said. "If you wanted."

"But I don't want to." Did she? No, definitely not. "I can't. Not after what he did. I'd look like a doormat. Letting him walk all over me and then come back when he's ready, it would be… embarrassing."

"But if you loved him…" Charlene's voice trailed off. She gave Annette a sad smile. "Love doesn't disappear just because someone doesn't deserve it. Believe me, I know."

Annette knew Charlene was talking about her daughter. Margaret's addictions had led her to lie and steal and even abandon her son on Charlene's doorstep. Now, Charlene was raising Tyler as her own, but she still mourned the loss of Margaret. Still hoped Margaret would clean up and turn her life around. She still loved her.

But that was different; that was flesh and blood. Annette had no idea if she had the same kind of enduring love for Frederick. The only thing she knew for sure was that his betrayal still hurt like it had the day she'd found out.

"Is it time to get a turtle?" A little voice sounded from the bottom of the stairs. Tyler.

He'd only been up in his room for twenty minutes—nowhere near long enough to be considered a good nap, but longer than any "nap" he'd taken in the last three weeks. Nap time was about to be a thing of the past, but Annette and Charlene were both determined to eke every last second out of it that they could.

Annette wiped at her eyes, surprised to find the beginnings of tears gathered there. She turned around and smiled at her nephew. "You're supposed to be asleep."

"I'm too excited to sleep! I want to get my turtle."

She'd completely forgotten about her promise to take Tyler to buy him a pet turtle for his birthday. Frederick's appearance had wiped everything else from her mind.

"Honey, you need to nap first," Charlene intervened.

Tyler crossed his arms defiantly. "But it's my birthday. I'm big now. I'm four."

"You still need a nap."

"I'm not sleepy."

"Tyler, please—"

"I'm awake," he insisted. "I'm not sleepy."

Charlene sighed. "Tyler, Aunt Net isn't feeling very good. Maybe we could do the turtle later?"

"But she promised." His wide hazel eyes went watery. "Aunt Net, you promised."

Annette had always been a sucker for those sad eyes. Even if she was currently uncertain of her ability to stand or speak or so much as breathe without dissolving into tears, she had to try. "I know, bud.

Just, uh, let me grab my—"

Suddenly, Noah jumped up and crossed the room to kneel in front of Tyler. "What if you and I go down to the beach? The pet store is closed right now," he lied easily. "But when it opens later, we'll come back and Aunt Net will take you. Is that okay?"

Tyler thought about it for a moment. Then the lure of the beach won him over, as it always did. "Can Sheldon come?"

"Let me get him from the laundry room." Charlene went to grab Tyler's stuffed turtle out of the dryer. After a trip to the beach, he'd need yet another "bath" in the washer. It was a wonder the poor creature hadn't disintegrated yet.

Charlene and Noah got Tyler ready for a trip to the beach while Annette slouched over her coffee in the kitchen. By the time the boys were out the door and Charlene had settled into the chair across from her, the coffee was cold. Annette hadn't taken a single sip of it.

"You don't have to take him to get the turtle if you don't want," Charlene said.

"You're only saying that because you don't want him to have a pet turtle in the first place."

"It was an outrageous gift to give a four-year-old. And if you leave, that turtle is going with you. I'm not cleaning up after it."

"I don't think turtles require much cleaning," Annette said. "And why would I leave?"

Charlene blinked. "I don't know."

"I'm not going with Frederick, if that's what you mean."

"I didn't mean anything," she lied. "But if you did want to go with him…"

"I don't!" She finally took a sip of the cold coffee and then pushed the mug away. "He has a baby. I know it sounds dumb, but I just realized that. Like, *realized* realized that. I knew his girlfriend was pregnant, but… she had the baby. He is a dad."

The words lodged in her throat. She'd tried so hard to make Frederick a father. The IVF treatments were draining, all those shots and pills and doctor's appointments. And now he had what he'd always wanted —what *they'd* always wanted… with someone else.

"I'm sorry," Charlene whispered.

"I wonder if that's why he cheated. Because I couldn't—because we never—" She swallowed. "He wanted kids. Maybe he realized the only way he'd ever get any is if he—"

Charlene reached across the table and grabbed Annette's forearm. "No. Cut that out right now. There is no excuse, Annette. None. What he did to you, it has nothing to do with you and everything to do with him."

Annette wanted to believe that. Part of her did believe it. But deep down, she still wondered.

"But you do need to figure out what you want," Charlene said. "He's going to come back. We both know he was serious when he said he'd stick around until the two of you could talk."

"He is annoyingly persistent."

Charlene nodded. "He's the only person in the world capable of getting us all to agree to listen to NPR on a cross-country road trip. As if traveling to go to Aunt Bev's funeral wasn't bad enough."

Annette smiled at the memory. "I thought Davy was going to die of boredom."

Annette could still picture Charlene's husband rolling his eyes and giving up the fight over the radio. The moment of levity was fleeting, but it left Annette feeling nauseous. A kind of emotional motion sickness.

She groaned and dropped her head in her hands. "I hate this."

Charlene lurched up and lifted Annette out of her chair. She pushed her towards the garage door. "You need to clear your head."

"In the garage?" Annette was too weak to resist her sister's shoving. She let herself be towed along, as helpless as a buoy on the waves.

"Go for a ride," she said. "You'll feel better."

Annette looked down at herself. "I'm in a dress. And sandals."

Charlene grabbed the bike helmet from the hook next to the door and pushed it against Annette's chest. "We both know you have bike shorts on under that dress. Go for a ride and clear your head."

Before Annette realized what was happening, she'd tied up the bottom of her green sundress around her thighs and strapped her helmet on. It was easier than thinking of reasons not to do it.

She slipped out of the garage and followed the path she took each morning, cruising past houses she'd seen a hundred times, a thousand times. Broad-hipped roofs slanting over deep, shady porches. Some mornings, Annette was awake enough to wave to neighbors drinking coffee or sipping sweet tea in the afternoons. But she kept her eyes on her front tire today. She didn't want to see anyone.

Which made it even more curious that she ended up at Front Beach. This deep in the summer, the shopping area was overrun with tourists Annette had to dodge. She nearly took out one woman who was too busy taking a picture of her ice cream cone to realize she was in the middle of the bike path.

"Excuse me!" Annette barked, too annoyed to be very polite. She swerved hard onto the sidewalk to avoid the woman and accidentally bumped a chalkboard bistro sign with her tire.

Grumbling under her breath, she dismounted quickly and picked the sign up to set it back in place. As she did, she read the neat lettering.

Grand Opening Special: BOGO Half Off Appetizers

She glanced up and realized the vacant building that until recently had served fresh-pressed health juices was now a cute little bistro. *Front Beachtro* according to the reflective metal sign above the door. Annette smiled at the play on words.

But she wasn't hungry for food or for human interaction. A herd of Midwesterners came trundling down the sidewalk just then, plowing between her and the bistro. She sighed and threw a leg back over her back.

The crowds down towards the heart of Front Beach looked even thicker and more oblivious, so Annette turned onto a side street and headed for home.

The ride had helped Annette reclaim control of her body. But her mind? Her heart? That was another beast entirely.

Pulling her bike back into the garage at Charlene's house, Annette had no more an idea of what she wanted to do than when she'd left. Frederick would come again. She'd have to talk to him.

But it was anyone's guess what she'd have to say.

2

NEXT DAY AT THE BEACH

No one was better at distraction than a four-year-old.

"Look, Aunt Net, a starfish!"

"Aunt Net, my boat sunk!"

"Make footprints in the sand with me, Aunt Net!"

Annette trudged along behind her nephew, wondering if she shouldn't have just gone to work.

The run-in with Frederick had settled in her body like too much cheap wine, and Annette had woken up feeling hungover. She was sluggish, mentally and physically, and she knew she wouldn't be of any use to anyone. She'd left a message with the Hunley Park Elementary front office telling Janice she wouldn't be in today.

Eleanor would be disappointed. She was a fourth grader with perfect diction, but no volume control. And even though Annette tried not to have favorites, Eleanor was definitely a favorite. Mostly because speech intervention with Eleanor was playing Whisper Tea Party or Whisper/Shout Karaoke. It was a nice break in the day from flash cards and exercises for tongue mobility.

But instead of sipping tea and whispering made-up gossip about their fellow tea partiers (all stuffed animals, yet Eleanor seemed to know an awful lot about who they did and didn't like), Annette was jogging down the beach, chasing a four-year-old who was currently wearing her cover-up knotted around his throat like a superhero cape.

Annette was exhausted. And like every other bad thing in her life lately, she blamed Frederick.

"Can Aunt Net take a break?" She rolled out a beach towel and dropped down onto her back. "I can't keep up."

"I'll slow down. See?" Tyler mimed running in slow motion, sound effects and all.

"Just a few minutes, and I'll be back and ready to play."

Tyler thought about it and then held up three fingers and a thumb. "Three minutes."

"Three minutes," Annette agreed.

Aunt Net didn't usually need breaks. When she and Tyler were together, it was full-on, non-stop playtime. But today, she didn't have as much to give as she usually did. Before going to bed, she'd unblocked Frederick's number from her phone. Now, it rang at least once an hour. And with every call, Annette felt her willpower slipping away.

Part of her wanted to block it again. Ignore him. Pretend he didn't exist.

But he *did* exist. And at some point, she'd have to talk with him. But what was there to say that hadn't already been said?

When Annette had found the notecard wedged beneath Frederick's cufflink box in his top drawer, she'd almost dropped to her knees. The proof was pressed to the paper, a plump lip print in a gaudy shade of pink Annette would never wear.

Immediately, she'd wanted to hunt for more evidence, but Frederick worked in IT. His computer and phone and accounts were locked down like Fort Knox. Plus, Annette didn't need any more proof. She knew in her heart what it was and what it meant.

When Frederick came home from his alleged "board game night" that evening, Annette threw the wadded-up notecard at him. "How could you?"

She didn't actually want to know, but Frederick answered, anyway.

She was a temp at our office.

I was just trying to be friendly.

I didn't mean for things to go this far.

"How far have things gone?" Annette asked. "How long?"

Frederick ran a hand over his stubble. "… Three years."

He'd jumped to explain himself, imbuing his explanation with more passion than Annette had gotten from him in months. Years, even. Her usually reserved, even-keeled husband flailed his arms and shed tears. Annette half-expected him to tear at his clothes and wail like a Victorian widow.

But she didn't hear any of it. Instead, Annette had run through three years' worth of memories. The anniversary when Frederick had surprised her with tickets to see *A Chorus Line* during its national tour. The trip they'd taken to Acadia National Park. Annette had a picture of them kissing on a mountain top framed and sitting on her desk at work. Every single day when he'd left for work, kissed her on the cheek, and said he loved her.

For three entire years, he'd been cheating on her.

"I love you, Annette. I do," he'd insisted. "But I love her, too. I can't help it. And I can't leave her. It wouldn't be right."

"Strange sense of loyalty considering you had no trouble cheating on me," she'd snapped.

"It's different. She's pregnant."

And that was it. Those few little words had said it all.

She's more important.

She gave me what you couldn't.

He couldn't leave his girlfriend because she was carrying his child. But Annette? She was only his wife. *Just* his wife.

"Has it been three minutes yet?" Tyler called from behind a misshapen drip sandcastle.

"It's been thirty seconds," Annette yelled back. She didn't actually know how long it had been, but she wasn't ready to get up just yet.

He sighed dramatically and went back to shoring up a crumbling wall.

Annette laid back and closed her eyes. The sun tinted the inside of her eyelids a pleasant, glowing tangerine.

No matter what Charlene thought Frederick's motives were, Annette knew the truth. They had nothing left to discuss. Frederick had been unwilling to leave his girlfriend when she was pregnant. And now, she'd had his baby. The child he'd always wanted.

He wouldn't leave either of them.

And Annette would never ask him to. Because as much as the reality of it felt like a knife to the chest, Annette understood.

Tyler was only her nephew, but she'd never abandon him. Not the way his own mother had. She couldn't even imagine it. Her world without him would be infinitely less rich. Just as Frederick's would be without his child.

An exaggerated groan pierced through her thoughts. "Aunt Net, it's too tough. Has it been three minutes?"

Annette smiled and hauled herself to her feet. "Yes, bud. It's been three minutes."

"You can come help me now!" he cheered.

Tyler scooped sand into the bucket and then handed it to Annette. It was her job to pack the sand down, upend the bucket, and then make sure every edge came out perfectly crisp. If it didn't, Tyler would declare it "wrecked" and demolish the entire thing to start over.

"Quite the perfectionist today, aren't we?"

Tyler looked at her, uncertainty in his wide eyes. "Huh?"

"It means you want things to be perfect. To look really good," she explained.

"Oh," he said. "I want this to look really, really good. It's gotta be the best sandcastle in the world."

"In that case, I better step up my game," she said.

They worked in concentrated silence for a long time. Really, it was only a minute or two. But for a four-year-old, it may as well have been an eternity.

Then Annette's phone rang. She had it strapped to her bicep using the workout band she wore while riding her bike, mostly in case Charlene or the school tried to get in touch with her. But when she unstrapped it and checked, she realized it was none of the above.

Just a familiar picture accompanying a familiar name she never wanted to see again.

She dismissed Frederick's call and shoved the phone back in the strap. A sinking feeling settled in her stomach. An internal quicksand that sucked at her, pulling more and more of her down into the depths. If it kept up like this, there'd be nothing left.

"Why did you get mad?"

Annette looked up and found Tyler staring at her. His little body was still, all of his attention fixed on her.

She pasted on a smile. "I'm not mad."

"You made a mad sound."

"I did?"

Tyler inhaled deeply and released a sharp sigh. "Like that."

Oh. Annette realized he was right. Tyler seemed to pick up on everything.

"I guess I am a little mad. But not at you."

"Who at?" He went back to scooping sand into his bucket.

"Someone you don't know."

"I know Grandma. And Noah," he said. "And Ms. Elaine."

"I'm not mad at any of them. It's another friend of mine."

"Who?"

This time when she sighed, she was very aware of it. "A special friend of mine. His name is Frederick."

"Fred-er-ick," Tyler said slowly. "Can I know him?"

"I'm not sure." It was better to be honest. Tyler remembered everything. If she told him he could meet Frederick, he'd ask her about it every day until it happened.

Tyler stood up and brushed the sand from his hands. "I have an idea. Frederick is your friend, so you can ask him to come play. When he gets here, I'll say, 'Hi.' Then we'll be friends."

What a world Tyler lived in. Where every friendship was a 'hello' and a playdate away.

"That's a great plan," Annette assured him, "but the problem is, Frederick and I aren't really friends right now."

His brow creased. "Why not?"

"He hurt my feelings." *Understatement of a lifetime.*

"Did he say he was sorry?" he asked. "Grandma says I have to 'pologize if I'm naughty."

Another confounding element of Tyler's world: no mistake was so large an apology couldn't fix it. What a place. What a life.

"He did apologize, but he really hurt my feelings. I'm not sure I can be friends with him again."

"That's not nice, Aunt Net."

Annette pressed a hand to her chest. "Me? I'm not being nice?"

He nodded. "He says, 'Sorry' and you say, 'Forgiven.' That's what Grandma says you're supposed to do."

She knew Tyler saw the world in a binary. There were good guys and bad guys, superheroes and villains. Surely real life had far more shades of gray. And yet, Annette couldn't help but wonder if Tyler wasn't right. Could it be as simple as he thought? If Frederick was genuinely sorry, could she just… forgive him?

Annette didn't know for sure, but she knew one thing: relying on her four-year-old nephew for therapy and marital counseling was a bad idea. Time for a distraction.

"Oh no!" she gasped dramatically.

Tyler snapped his attention to her. "What? What?"

"We forgot something for the castle!"

He stood up, ready to sprint in whichever direction she pointed. "What?"

"Seashells!"

"Seashells!" he shouted as he ran in a circle. "We forgot seashells!"

Together, they combed the beach and dug through the sand. Annette tucked all of their favorite seashells into the pockets of her cover-up. And as the sun moved across the sky and her phone continued to ring again and again, she could no longer remember who was supposed to be distracting who.

3

A FEW DAYS LATER AT CHARLENE'S HOUSE

"I can't believe he is still asleep," Charlene said.

Annette snorted over her laptop. "That's because you weren't on that bike ride with us this morning."

Thursdays were Annette's short days. Aside from a quick speech therapy session at Burns Elementary just before lunch, the rest of her day was lesson planning, which she liked to do from home. Preferably in her pajamas.

Today, she'd opted to take Tyler with her on her morning ride. She'd expected him to make it halfway around the block and want to go home, but that kid hung with her for two miles. It was a surprise his training wheels hadn't ground down to the rims.

"It's been two hours. Two. Hours," Charlene repeated in awe. "Can you take him on a ride every day?"

"Only if you're willing to pay me a full-time nanny fee. Because I'd have to quit my job."

Charlene wrinkled her nose. "I guess it's the 'no nap' lifestyle for us then. Darn."

Annette sipped her third coffee of the day. More than enough caffeine zipped through her veins, but she still felt haggard. "Kids have no idea how good they have it. I'd nap all the time if I could."

"I wouldn't. I hate naps," Charlene said. "But I saw your light still on when I got up to take Tyler to the bathroom. You probably do need a nap."

"I'm okay. I just haven't been sleeping well."

Charlene reached across the table and snapped Annette's laptop closed.

"Hey!" she protested. "What if I hadn't saved?"

"Did you?"

"… Yes."

"Then quit complaining. You need to stop ducking things and do it."

"Do what?"

"Call him," Charlene said.

Annette shoved her sister's hand away and opened her laptop. "I don't know what you're talking about."

"Don't be hard-headed."

"Don't be nosey," Annette fired back.

"I'm not trying to be nosey. I'm trying to be a good sister," she said. "Clearly, Frederick being in town is bothering you. Put yourself out of your misery. Talk to him!"

Right on cue, Annette's phone buzzed. It was as if Frederick could tell they were talking about him. Annette was convinced she could say his name three times into a mirror and he'd appear behind her like Beetlejuice.

She swiped away to dismiss the call. "I'll talk to him… eventually."

"When?" Charlene asked. "Before you drop of exhaustion, I hope?"

"Soon, okay? I'll call him soon."

Annette's phone immediately started buzzing again, and Charlene pursed her lips. "I want you to talk to him for your sake, Ann. Not his."

With that, Charlene stood up and left Annette alone, staring at the ringing phone.

Her finger hovered over the screen. Annette wasn't sure which way to swipe. It felt like diffusing a bomb. Should she cut the red wire or the blue wire? Swipe up or down? Up and she'd have to formulate actual words to the man who broke her heart, which felt far beyond her current capabilities. Down and she'd endure yet another anxious day and sleepless night, wondering what Frederick wanted to say to her.

Was the devil she knew better than the devil she didn't?

Before she could convince herself otherwise, Annette swiped up and said hello to the devil.

"What is it, Frederick?"

"Annie! I can't believe you answered."

"I can't believe it, either," she said. "Talk fast before I start to regret my decision."

"Go to dinner with me."

"Is that a question or a command?"

"It's a plea," he said.

"Plea denied. Just say what you need to say."

"It's not that simple," Frederick said. "You and I have big discussions over dinner. Always have. Since the very beginning."

A movie reel flickered suddenly in Annette's mind.

Frederick sat across from her at a chain Italian restaurant, decades younger in a crewneck sweatshirt with a collared shirt layered underneath. She had on a black slip dress with spaghetti straps that she'd borrowed from Charlene. The waiter seemed to appreciate it. The minute he wrote down their orders, Frederick reached across the table and grabbed her hand.

"I wanted to wait until the food came. I thought maybe if your mouth was full you wouldn't be able to refuse me."

"Refuse you what?" she laughed.

Frederick swallowed nervously. "I want to know if you'll be my girlfriend. My exclusive, one and only girlfriend."

Annette's heart fluttered. "Is there another kind?"

"Not to me. But I want to make sure I'm explicit," he said.

This was their first date. Annette had only known Frederick for a few weeks. But she didn't have a doubt in the world when she bit her bottom lip and nodded. "Sure. I'll be your girlfriend."

Frederick leaned across the table and tipped her chin up. For some strange reason, Annette felt like Cinderella's glass slipper. The way Frederick handled her made her feel priceless. Magical. When they kissed, it was just a soft brush of lips, but Annette felt it in her toes.

"Wow," Frederick sighed when he dropped back down on his side of the booth. Then he grinned. "Maybe you can call me your boyfriend or something when the waiter comes back? It might make me petty, but I want to rub it in."

Annette tipped her head back and laughed...

And the tape cut. The screen went black. Annette blinked and she was back in the present moment, a phone pressed to her ear. Older and wiser, but perhaps a little more tired in her bones than she once was.

"You only insisted we talk over dinner because I get grouchy when I'm hungry," she said. "And luckily, I just ate a blueberry muffin. So talk."

"I'm sorry, Annie, but it's dinner or I keep calling until you agree."

Annette stretched back in her chair. Her body creaked and twinged like she'd aged twenty years in the last four days. "I can block your number again, you know."

"Go to dinner with me and that will be the end of it. Scout's honor."

They hadn't been together in almost a year. Any sane person would say their relationship had ended long before now. Still, hearing the words come out of Frederick's mouth made Annette flinch.

"What does that mean?"

"It means, sit down and talk to me. After that, I won't ask for your forgiveness again. This is my last stand. Like Custer."

"Custer died in his last stand."

"Did he?"

"Yes. In the Battle of Little Bighorn."

"Hm. Well, that's a risk I'm willing to take." He paused. "Is that you agreeing?"

Frederick sounded so normal. So calm. That wasn't a surprise, really. Except for the conversation where he'd admitted he loved another woman, Frederick maintained an even tone at all times. But it did make it hard for Annette to remember their new dynamic: the Scorner and the Scorned.

"I guess you won't leave me alone until I do."

"You know me. Persistent," he said.

Yes, Annette did know him. Unfortunately, he wasn't easy to forget.

"Tonight. Seven. I'll pick the restaurant and text you." Then she hung up.

❧

Annette scrolled through an endless list of restaurants on her phone and groaned. "I feel like a kid picking the switch they're going to get whipped with."

"You're not going for the food. Pick any place," Charlene said. "Pick somewhere with an easily accessible fire exit, maybe."

"What if this is like when you throw up after eating a certain food and then you can't ever eat it again?"

Italian food was off limits. She didn't need any more walks down memory lane. Maybe Mexican? No, cream cheese chicken enchiladas were her comfort food. She couldn't let Frederick spoil them.

"Hm, good point." Charlene frowned in thought and then shivered. "Belgian Waffles for me. Especially if there's whipped cream involved. Makes me nauseous just thinking about it."

"I don't want to eat something I like tonight and then associate it with him forever."

"But what if it's a good association?" Charlene offered.

Annette glared at her sister over her phone, though Charlene was too busy rifling through Annette's closet to notice.

"It won't be. Trust me," she said.

Charlene whirled around, a dark blue wrap dress in her hands. "This dress with your brown sandals. And I have that necklace—"

"The knotted gold chain? That will look perfect." Annette sighed, then it curdled into a grimace. "Do I want to look perfect, though? I don't want him to think I care."

"But you do care. Otherwise you wouldn't be so worried."

Annette flopped back on the bed. "This is ridiculous. I'm not a twenty-year-old kid anymore. I shouldn't be obsessing over every little detail like this. It's not even a date."

"I go through this same process every time I go out with Noah. It's normal."

"Nothing about this is normal." She sighed again, then added, "Do you know, for our last wedding anniversary, we just ordered Pad Thai and rented a movie? I don't even remember which movie. *No need to make a fuss after all these years*, we said. Just saying that now makes me crazy. We got kind of... boring. Do you think that's why—"

"Every couple gets boring," Charlene said. "At least a little bit. Human beings aren't built for constant excitement. It's why we settle down. At some point, you stop drinking too much and have a self-enforced bedtime."

"And eat bran cereal with skim milk."

"Exactly," she said. "Well, you do that, not me. But if your life was nonstop excitement and Frederick still cheated, you'd be sitting here wondering if you should have had more nights in. If you should have cuddled more."

"So you're saying it was inevitable?"

"I'm saying," Charlene dropped down onto the bed and wrapped her arm around Annette's shoulders, "this was Frederick's decision. It had nothing to do with what you did or didn't do."

"You really think so? You can be honest."

After everything she'd been through, Annette craved honesty. Even if it was harsh.

"I do. Frederick messed up. It's why he wants you back."

Annette wagged a warning finger. "We don't know that."

"*You* don't know that," Charlene corrected. "But I do. Why else would he want to talk about?"

"Maybe he wants to ask me to be his child's godmother," Annette joked.

"Can you imagine?"

Annette shrugged. "Maybe he'll make me an offer I can't refuse."

They both laughed, and Annette felt ever-so-slightly better. Frederick had devastated her before, and she'd moved on. She'd found a new job, reconnected with her sister, met her nephew. Good things had come after Frederick. It had happened once; it could happen again. No matter what he had to say to her.

After they caught their breath, Charlene stood up and helped Annette to her feet. "Do your makeup, wear this blue dress, and go eat some curry."

"Ew. I hate curry."

"Exactly," Charlene winked. "He can't ruin something you already hate."

Annette pulled her sister into a bone-crushing hug. "Thanks, Char."

Evening At Indian Restaurant

"I thought you hated curry." Frederick leaned back, one arm draped over the back of the booth.

"I used to. But things change."

No, they certainly didn't. Not in this case, at least—coconut milk still made her stomach turn. But Frederick didn't need to know that. In some ways, it felt good to see him reach for something familiar and miss. He couldn't pretend he knew everything about her now.

He gave her a tight smile. "I heard you're teaching again."

"Where did you hear that?"

"From the intense internet search I did a few months ago," he admitted. "Your name was on the Charleston County School District's staff directory. How is that going?"

"Fine."

He nodded awkwardly. "I bet you're good at that. You're more patient than I am. And better with kids."

"You're the dad," she said coldly.

The conversation once again flopped to the table like a dead fish. Frederick sighed. "I want to wait until the food comes."

"For what?" she asked, even though she already knew.

"You know."

To talk. To explain himself. He wanted to wait until her mouth was full, so she wouldn't refuse whatever he wanted to ask her quite as quickly.

But it was hard to talk about anything else when that topic still lingered. Their shared history wrapped around them like an itchy wool blanket, uncomfortable and stifling.

Frederick leaned forward, and Annette looked at him. Really *looked* at him for the first time in ten months. Since arriving at Taste of India, she'd been staring just past his shoulder, just over his head. Doing her best to guard herself against the familiar, pained eyes that were staring at her now.

"Can we just… talk?" he asked. "Please? Just have a conversation with me. Forget for a second that you hate my guts, and talk to me."

"I don't hate your guts." The words tumbled out before she could stop them. They were true, but that didn't mean she'd had any intention of saying them. Even when she was mad at Frederick, she wanted to comfort him. Even when he didn't deserve it, she couldn't help but care.

"You don't?"

This felt like a slippery slope into a conversation Annette wasn't ready to have. She folded her hands on the table in front of her. "Are you still working at the accounting firm?"

A smile flickered across his face. "Head of IT now. Patrick is in my old position."

"I'm sure he hates that."

"He does," Frederick laughed. "Being a millennial and growing up with the internet doesn't make him smarter than me."

"Can you tell that to a girl I work with? She talks to me like I'm ninety every time I tell her the printer in the front office isn't working." Annette shifted her voice several octaves higher and spoke painfully slowly. *"Did... you... select... the... right... printer?'* 'Yes, Morgan, I did. I print out things at fifteen different schools and never have issues. It's just your dumb printer.'"

Frederick laughed. "I'll be sure to send the memo to Patrick and Morgan."

"Thank you," Annette smiled.

She was still smiling when she looked up at Frederick for the second time. Suddenly, the blanket around them felt a bit more comfortable. Less overwhelming. Which put Annette immediately on edge.

That's how quickly she could slip back into things as normal with Frederick. Just a second of letting her guard down and he'd wormed his way back in, made her smile, put her at ease the way he always had.

Did he and his girlfriend have the same easy rapport?

Annette shifted her gaze over his shoulder. Red light from the restaurant's neon sign glowed across the glass so Annette couldn't see out. It was just a reflection of the restaurant. A never-ending stretch of tables and diners and coconut-based foods.

Before she could jump out of the booth and make a run for it, the waitress arrived with their food. She slid bowls of red curry in front of each of them.

"You folks enjoy your food. Is there anything else I can do for you?"

Point me to the nearest emergency exit, maybe? thought Annette.

"This will be all," Frederick said. "Thanks."

Charlene was a genius. Annette was so tied up in knots about what Frederick would say to her, she felt sick. She couldn't imagine taking a single bite of anything, curry or otherwise. Coming here was a great decision.

"Are you going to eat?" Frederick took a bite. "It's good."

"The food is here. You said you wanted to wait until the food was here, and it's here. What do you need to say?"

He sighed. Annette held onto the sound precisely because it grated so much. She wanted to remember everything that had ever been wrong with their relationship.

Strangely, in their time apart, it had been easier to remember the good times than the bad. But she had to make herself actively work to remember the things that annoyed her and upset her. The things she did that annoyed and upset him. Annette needed to recall all of the things that love had made it easy to overlook. It was the only way she'd make it out of Taste of India with her dignity intact.

Frederick sat down his spoon. "I suppose I should be grateful you showed up at all. And that you took my call."

"Mhmm."

"Thank you for taking my call," he continued. "After what I did, the way I treated you, I... I don't know what to say."

"There's nothing to say."

"'I'm sorry' is a start."

"You already said that," she snapped. "You apologized the night it happened. Or the night I found out, anyway. We've already done this."

"But I mean it. I *meant* it. Then and now. I am so truly sorry, Annie."

She ground her teeth together. "Stop calling me that."

Frederick frowned. "It's what I've always called you."

"You used to be faithful to me, too. Clearly, things change." She took a deep breath. "Whatever you want, just ask for it, okay? I don't want your money or the house. I'll sign whatever you want me to sign. Just… just spit it out so I can go."

Annette could feel him staring at her. Disappointment emanated from him like static electricity. But she didn't care, wouldn't care, couldn't care. She needed this to be over.

"I hate that things are like this between us," he said finally. "I hate that we… aren't us anymore."

"That's your fault."

"I know." He dipped his head. "God, do I know it. I messed everything up, and… I wish I could take it back. I want to take it back."

Annette stilled. What did that mean? What was Frederick trying to say? The truth was a wild bear sitting between them and she was terrified to poke it.

Frederick kept going even without encouragement from her. "I know things can't go back to the way they were. But I hope, maybe, we could start something new. The two of us."

Something new. Not what they had before. "Are you asking me if I want to be friends?"

"No!" he said quickly. "Well, in a way, yes. You and I have always been friends. Best friends. And I want that with you again." He took a deep breath. "I'm saying this all wrong."

"Then just say it," Annette said. She was growing weary of the not-knowing.

He nodded. "Okay, you're right. I'll just say it. I left Debbie."

Debbie. Annette had done her best not to look into who Frederick had cheated on her with, but she couldn't help herself. Debbie Wilkening. Blonde and blue. Studying to be a dental hygienist. Mother of Frederick's child.

"You left her?"

"Yes. I left her," he repeated. "For you."

Annette blinked at him. "Charlene was right."

He opened his mouth to say something. But before he could, Annette grabbed her purse and left.

4

FRIDAY AT FRONT BEACHTRO

Charlene had been wrong. So, so wrong.

According to her older sister, talking to Frederick was supposed to help Annette relax and finally get some sleep. Why, then, had she spent the entire night staring at her ceiling, replaying his words over and over again in her head?

I left her. For you.

It was the most confusing earworm ever.

He left Annette for Debbie and now he was looking for a return. Really, how many times was he going to play this game of back-and-forth?

Not again, if Annette's pride had anything to say about it. For three years, Frederick had cheated on her. And she'd been gone ten months before he realized his mistake. She had her dignity. She could not take him back.

… But his apology seemed sincere. Maybe he'd cheated on her for three years without ending their marriage because he truly couldn't live without her. It wasn't a morally sound argument, but it had a tinge of romance to it, if she squinted and tilted her head to the side and didn't think about it too hard.

Would she really deny herself a possible second chance at love because of something as silly as pride?

Maybe.

Maybe not.

Probably not.

But maybe.

By the time the sun came up, Annette was exhausted and restless. She called into work sick for the second time that week and left for a bike ride before Tyler or Charlene could wake up. She wasn't ready to talk to anyone about what had happened yet, mostly because she still wasn't quite sure herself.

Stars were still visible overhead even as the sun was starting to cook away the dark. The balmy air felt like a warm sweater against Annette's skin and there wasn't a cloud in the sky. She could already tell it was going to be a perfect summer day.

"Morning, honey," called a familiar from the beach access path. Elaine had her usual jumbo-sized travel mug of coffee. "Getting a jump on the day? I don't usually see you for another hour."

Elaine took a walk every morning. Occasionally, if Annette peeled herself out of bed early enough, she'd pass Elaine on her way back home, coffee cup dangling empty at her side. Today, Elaine was just walking out of her front gate. Annette could see the steam spiraling out of her mug.

Annette slowed down but kept pedaling. "I got an early start today."

More like she'd had a late night, but... technicalities. Elaine would probably know the truth of it soon. Eventually, her walk would loop back around to the beach in front of Charlene's house, and she'd run in to Charlene and Tyler on their morning walk. The two women loved their daily gossip sessions. Annette knew Elaine would hear all about Frederick before the morning dew could evaporate.

So she waved goodbye and kept riding. She didn't much feel like chatting anyway.

Once again, she found herself headed towards Front Beach. Thankfully, it was early in the day, well before peak tourist hours. Most of the shops weren't open yet, but she could stop in for her favorite ham and egg breakfast sandwich at Café Paname. Or was it possible the residual side effects of her dinner with Frederick could ruin her breakfast, too?

Better not risk it, she thought, and took a left towards the beach. Then she smelled something that stopped her in her tracks.

Annette skidded to a stop and turned towards the delectable scent of hot coffee and bacon. It was coming from the little bistro she'd seen a few days earlier, Front Beachtro. And like a shark to blood, Annette couldn't resist. She chained up her bike and went in.

Front Beachtro was deceptively large inside. The space was narrow but deep. A wooden bench ran along the right wall with small two-tops spaced evenly down its length. Larger, four-person tables were scattered across the glossy concrete floor.

"Just one today?" The hostess had a smile brighter than the still-rising sun. Annette hoped she was being paid well to be that cheerful so early in the morning.

"Just me," she confirmed.

She was led to one of the small tables in the corner, which was nice. It let her peruse the early morning crowd.

Two men in suits sat on the edge of their chairs near the front of the restaurant, checking their watches. When a woman came out holding a pair of to-go bags, they jumped up, grabbed them, and hurried for the door. Annette wasn't in nearly the same rush.

She ordered a water and a coffee to start from the beaming hostess. Then Annette was left alone to peruse the modest but delicious-looking menu. She was still torn between a cheddar cheese and scallion scone or a turkey sausage and smoked gouda quiche when her waiter arrived.

"Ready to order?"

Annette looked up and smiled. This day just kept getting better. Her waiter looked like an actual prince. Auburn, wavy hair, a friendly smile, and broad shoulders that looked capable of conveying a devastating amount of breakfast foods from the kitchen directly to her mouth.

"I'm torn between a scone and a quiche. Do you know which is best?"

"Ahh, I can't pick. Both are great options."

"Yeah, but which one is better?" She lowered her voice to a whisper and added, "I promise I won't tell your boss you said anything bad about the food."

He chuckled, a deep, warm sound. "Well, considering I am the boss, I'd say the cat's already out of the bag."

She pulled back and looked the man over. He had on fitted khaki pants and a white pocket tee. Not exactly business formal, but certainly crisp and put-together. Most notably, he wasn't wearing the same black button-down shirt with the bistro's logo stitched over the breast that the rest of the staff was wearing. That should have been a clue.

"Oh." Annette's face flushed. "I'm embarrassed."

"Don't be. How could you have known? We just opened." He held out his hand. "Gregory Dane."

Annette shook his hand, aware her palm was still clammy from her bike ride. "Annette… Campbell."

She'd almost given him her maiden name; but legally speaking, she was still tied to Frederick. And at this point, she'd been Campbell almost as long as she'd been Wilson.

"Nice to meet you, Annette."

"Same to you, Gregory. I actually almost met you the other day, I think. I was on a bike ride and saw the name. Front Beachtro. Genius."

He laughed. "You like that? Some people don't get it. And explaining a joke is a lot like dissecting a frog—"

"You understand it, but the frog dies in the process," Annette finished. "I love that quote."

"You were the intended audience for my taste in humor."

"And taste in food," she said, holding up the menu. "Everything looks delicious. I really can't decide what to get."

Gregory leaned down to study the menu. Annette could smell his soap —a spicy, woodsy scent. "Okay, if I'm being honest… my scones are better than my quiches."

"Is that right? Very forthcoming of you."

He held up his thumb and forefinger, a tiny sliver of space between them. "Just ever-so-slightly better. Both incredible—world-class, even. But one is more reliable than the other. I've been known to have a soggy bottom."

Annette practically choked on her coffee.

"On my pastry crust," Gregory said quickly. He ran a hand down his face. "Wow. Now I'm embarrassed. Did I just say that out loud?"

Annette stifled a laugh. "Don't be. Pastry is hard to work with. We all have a soggy bottom from time to time."

"I'm going to pretend that never happened. Now that I've filled your head with horrible imagery, do you know what you'd like to order?"

"I've heard your scones are more reliable, so I'll take one of those."

He took her menu with a grin. "One scone, coming right up."

Annette hid her smile in her coffee cup, feeling silly for being unable to wipe it off her face. But how often did you get to talk to a handsome man about pastry? In Annette's experience, never. And considering those were two of her favorite things, she counted herself very lucky.

She'd never made a quiche—savory bakes were more her sister's expertise—but she knew a lot about pastry crust. The first time she'd tried to make a caramel custard pie for the Thanksgiving potluck at Frederick's work, it had turned to soup. It took three tries before she realized she needed to pre-bake the crust to avoid it disintegrating in the liquid from the custard. Considering Gregory owned a bistro, he probably knew to blind bake his crust before filling it, but it couldn't hurt to offer a suggestion when he came back. Especially if it meant continuing their conversation.

Annette watched people come and go, picking up carryout orders for coffee and pastries or claiming a table and perusing the menu the way she'd done. A few people seemed to have been there before, but since the bistro was newly opened, most were there for the first time.

Annette had just met Gregory, but she found herself feeling strangely proud of him. Front Beachtro already had more traffic in its first week than she'd ever seen at The Green Way Juicery. Probably because they'd charged ten dollars for an eight-ounce concoction that tasted like a liquidated compost pile, whereas Annette could come here and get a delicious scone and a creamy latte for the exact same price. It was a no-brainer if ever there was one.

When Gregory came back, he had a plate in each hand. He sat down the first. "Your scone, and," he slid a second plate in front of her, "your quiche."

"But I only ordered the scone," she argued, even as her mouth watered at the sight of the golden brown, flaky pastry crust.

"Consider it payment for hearing about my soggy bottom." Gregory laughed. "And it sounded like maybe you've worked with pastry crust before? So, think of it as me putting you to work. I'd love a fellow baker's opinion."

"Home baker," Annette amended. "You're the one with a bistro. I should be getting advice from you."

He put his hands on his hips, broadening his already broad frame. Gregory looked every bit the charming heartthrob. She wondered if he was aware of just how good-looking he was when he grinned like that. "Anytime. I'd be happy to show you what goes on in the kitchen."

Was he asking her on a date? It had been a long time since Annette had flirted with anyone, and even longer since she'd been asked out on a first date. But she was pretty sure she still recognized the signs.

"The tables turned pretty quickly there," she teased. "First, you wanted tips and now you're offering baking classes?"

Gregory shrugged. "I'm just trying to be an accommodating business owner. The customer is always right, right?"

"Right."

"Then you just tell me what you want, and I'll offer it," he said smoothly. "Enjoy your breakfast. Oh, and come back soon?"

The question carried a little extra weight. A sense of anticipation. Annette had the feeling she'd be agreeing to more than just returning for a scone and a coffee. So, as Gregory backed away from the table, she smiled but didn't make any promises.

Though, if she'd taken a bite of the scone first, she would have promised Gregory Dane anything.

It was incredible. Crumbly and moist, stuffed with a perfect balance of cheese and scallions and seasonings. Annette was grateful Gregory had returned to the kitchen because she inhaled the scone in two seconds flat. As soon as she was done, she turned her attention to the quiche.

Like Gregory had warned her, the bottom of the crust was a little wet, but the sides were perfectly crisp and flaky. A lot of times, pastry crust was used as nothing more than a vehicle to get fillings in your mouth, but this crust was garlicky and delicious. Mr. Dane had a gift, and Front Beachtro had absolutely earned her money.

"Was everything to your liking?" a waitress asked as she cleared the two empty plates from the table.

"Everything was amazing," Annette said. She hesitated and then added, "Tell the owner to keep up the good work. I'll definitely be back again."

Gregory, unfortunately, was nowhere to be found by the time the check arrived. The bill only charged Annette for the scone, so she added the price of the quiche to her tip. Then she strolled through the front door and into the warm mid-morning.

Parents loaded down with strollers and wagons pulled children covered in sunscreen down the street and rental cars fought to parallel park on the narrow side roads, but Annette couldn't be bothered. Not by tourists or the fact that a seagull had left an unpleasant gift on her bike seat. Thanks to her delicious breakfast and the man who served it, Annette was floating.

She was halfway home, sweat dripping down her back and endorphins pumping through her veins, when she realized she hadn't thought about Frederick in an hour at least. After a sleepless night where he'd filled every thought, Gregory Dane had wiped him from her mind for a blessed sixty minutes.

Her smile stretched even wider. It stayed that way the rest of her ride home.

5

NEXT DAY AT FRONT BEACHTRO

Annette resisted going back to the bistro Saturday morning for breakfast. And for lunch, she made herself and Tyler macaroni and cheese with hotdogs. While eating the processed kiddie food, she only daydreamed about the kind of delicious lunch menu Gregory must have put together a few dozen times. But by dinner, she'd been riding solo with a four-year-old for half a dozen hours and needed a change of scenery.

So why not go see what Mr. Dane was cooking up?

"Are we gotta go inside?" Tyler asked, clinging to Annette's hand as they walked down the sidewalk in front of Front Beachtro.

"Yeah. We're going to go inside and eat."

"Is Grandma in there?"

"No, she's out with Noah." Annette had to be careful not to mention Charlene and Noah were out on Noah's boat for the day. Otherwise, she'd be in for one heck of a temper tantrum. The boy loved being out on the boat.

"It's just going to be the two of us," she said. *And maybe a handsome bistro owner, but who can say?* "Is that okay?"

"Yeah, that's okay, Aunt Net." He squeezed her hand tighter.

The same blonde hostess from the morning before greeted them at the door. She beamed down at Tyler. "Table for two? And will you need a booster seat?"

Annette started to answer, but Tyler cut her off. "I'm a big boy. I sit in chairs."

She cast an amused look at Annette for confirmation.

"You heard him," Annette laughed. "Just a table with two normal chairs, please."

"A little man who knows what he wants. I love to see it. Right this way."

As the woman led them through the restaurant, Annette couldn't help but look around for any sign of the owner. A small part of her hoped he wasn't there. She felt silly for coming back so soon after their first conversation. She didn't want to give Gregory the wrong idea. But a much bigger part of her wanted to talk to him again. The distraction had been nice, to say the least.

Tyler may have wanted to sit in a big boy chair, but he had no interest at all in the big boy menu. Annette read him the list of entrees, which included pork and mushroom ramen and black bean burgers, and he immediately asked if they could go somewhere else.

"We just got here, bud. And I think you'll like the food if you give it a try," she said.

He crossed his arms and set his lips in a thin line. "Nuh-uh. It's yucky."

"Come on, Tyler. They have chicken. You like chicken." She decided not to mention it was chicken cordon bleu. They could cross that bridge when they came to it.

"Yucky, Aunt Net. I don't want it."

"Uh-oh. Do I have a displeased customer?"

Annette recognized Gregory's voice instantly and turned around. He had on a navy-blue pair of slacks and light grey button down that made his red hair look even more vibrant. He was also carrying a coloring sheet and a small box of crayons. He looked like the Saint of Squirmy Children to Annette, and not a moment too soon.

Still, Tyler eyed the man suspiciously. Clearly, all of their conversations about stranger danger were finally beginning to stick.

"I'm afraid so," Annette said. "Might be a generational thing. He's a fan of the classics."

"Corndogs and grilled cheeses?" Gregory asked.

"And chicken nuggets shaped like dinosaurs. I'd say that covers all the hits."

Tyler sat up straight. "Are corndogs the ones with sticks?"

"Yeah. Remember the one you had at the roller rink?"

Charlene and Annette had taken Tyler to the roller rink for an afternoon, but they'd spent the day clinging to the walls so they wouldn't fall and break a hip. Tyler skated fearless circles around them.

His hazel eyes widened and he looked around the bistro. "Are we going to skate, too?"

"No. We're just here for dinner," Annette said.

"I'm afraid we couldn't fit a roller rink between all the tables and chairs," Gregory said. He spread the coloring sheet and crayons out on the table in front of Tyler. "But I can offer you a coloring page and a corn dog with French fries?"

Tyler nodded enthusiastically.

"You got it, buddy," Gregory winked. "And what about you, Annette? Do you know what you want or do you need another recommendation from me?"

He remembered her name. Annette's theory that maybe Gregory bantered with all of his customers and she wasn't special at all immediately went out the window.

"A recommendation sounds great, actually. I haven't had time to study the menu, anyway."

"That's because your son is a tough critic. But I respect that. It keeps me on my toes."

"Oh no." Annette draped an arm over Tyler's shoulders. "Not my son. This is my nephew, Tyler."

Tyler was so busy scribbling the horns of a cartoon dragon bright purple that he didn't even look up.

"Oh, jeez, I'm sorry. I just assumed," Gregory said. "I should know better by now. You know what they say about assuming."

"I do, but we have young ears nearby. I shouldn't say."

Gregory laughed. "Can you tell I don't have any kids? I don't know all of the rules."

"Tyler is the closest thing I have to a kid."

"He's alive and not crying, so you're doing better than I would be," he joked. "I don't even have siblings. So no nieces or nephews, either. When it comes to kids, I'm lost."

"It's easy," she said. "As far as the rules go, they're basically the opposite of gremlins: lots of sunlight and water. Though, the 'no food after midnight' rule holds true. If he's awake at midnight, something has gone terribly wrong."

Gregory threw his head back and laughed. "Wow. What a throwback. I haven't seen that movie in years. Decades, actually."

"I just thought of another rule," she added. "Don't let children watch *Gremlins*. I watched it for the first time when I was his age, and I'm still traumatized."

"Noted. I'll try to remember all of that. You know, if I randomly find myself in the company of a child."

She could swear there was a little extra something implied in the way he said that, but before she could puzzle it out, Tyler grabbed her shirt sleeve. "Look, Aunt Net! A dragon."

The coloring sheet was covered in a mess of loopy scribbles in every color of the rainbow. The black ink outline of the dragon was barely visible underneath the colorful scrawl. Annette had never seen anything more beautiful.

"Whoa! That's the coolest dragon I've ever seen, bud."

He held it up to his face and roared like a beast, giggling when Annette and Gregory both shrunk away in fear.

"I better go put these orders in before the dragon gets too hungry and starts eating customers," Gregory said. "I'll be back."

The back of the coloring sheet was a word search, which Tyler entertained himself with by drawing messy squares around each of the letters and scribbling them in different colors. Annette was content to watch him hard at work. By the time he finished the last letter, Gregory was cutting back through the restaurant with a tray held over his shoulder.

If it was strange for the owner to be personally delivering food to the customers, none of the waitstaff let it show. Did he do this regularly, she wondered?

"One corn dog with ketchup and French fries for the ravenous dragon," he said when he reached their table. "And for the pretty lady, gnocchi with roasted chicken and gorgonzola cream."

Annette's cheeks flushed at the compliment. "Wow, this looks amazing. But what's that?"

Gregory still had one more bowl left on the tray, and he smiled nervously. "Well, if it's not too forward of me, I'm actually on break right now. I thought maybe I could... join you two?"

Okay, that couldn't possibly be normal practice. How many customers could he realistically sit down and share a meal with throughout the day?

Well... three, she supposed. But that seemed unlikely. Maybe she and Tyler were getting special treatment. She shivered pleasantly and put the question of why that might be out of her mind.

"That's not too forward. It's just forward enough." Annette squeezed Tyler's shoulder. "What do you say, kiddo? Do you mind if he eats with us?"

"Is that Fred-er-ick?" Tyler asked without looking up.

Annette blanched.

Kids really do say the darnedest things.

She did her best to smile easily. Gregory certainly didn't need to know all of her baggage. After all, this was only their second... interaction. Not a date. She was a paying customer and she'd shown up without being invited. Hardly a date.

"No, buddy," she said as gently as she could. "This is Gregory. He owns the restaurant."

Between the question and Annette's answer, Tyler lost interest. He was peeling the breading off of his corndog and dropping it into his open mouth in chunks.

Annette smiled at Gregory and shook her head. "Please feel free to eat with us. We don't mind, I promise."

"Much obliged." Gregory settled into the chair next to Annette with his own bowl of gnocchi. "Is Frederick a friend of yours?"

"A special friend," Tyler said before Annette could stop him.

"Oh, is that right?" Gregory immediately looked like he regretted asking.

Annette's face was on fire. Her tongue felt swollen and clumsy in her mouth. So much for keeping her baggage to herself. "He's my ex-husband. Well, husband. But we are separated." She sighed. "It's complicated."

"Relationships often are." Gregory gave her a sympathetic smile and mercifully changed the subject. "Are you from Isle of Palms?"

"Yeah. Well, sort of," she said. "I lived in Asheville, North Carolina for fifteen years. But about a year ago, I moved back to IOP."

"Because of the complications?"

She chuckled awkwardly. "Correct. But what about you? Why'd you open a restaurant here?"

"I'm from Knoxville originally, but I went to the University of South Carolina. I spent a few spring breaks here over the years and loved it."

"Oh, you're a Gamecock?"

"Tried and true." He puffed out his chest. "You too?"

"Sorry to disappoint. I'm a Tiger."

"A Clemson girl. Okay, okay." Gregory blew on a bite of gnocchi, which reminded Annette she hadn't even touched her food. "I knew you had to have at least one flaw."

Again, Annette couldn't miss the implied compliment. "If being a Tiger is wrong, then I don't want to be right."

He laughed. "Fine. We'll have to agree to disagree, I suppose."

"I suppose," she said, smiling at him over her bowl.

Like the breakfast the morning before, the gnocchi was delicious. Tender, soft as a pillow, but with a good bite. And the cheese sauce was perfectly creamy. Annette needed the recipe. Either that, or she needed to kidnap the chef and force him to cook for her.

"This is so much better than macaroni and cheese with hotdogs," she sighed between bites.

"Nuh-uh!" Tyler argued. "I like hotdogs."

Gregory let out a low whistle. "That's a mighty high bar you're making me jump over, Annette."

"Are you intimidated by my culinary prowess?"

"Quaking in my boots," he teased. "You weren't kidding about those cooking lessons, were you?"

"And you weren't kidding about your soggy bottom," Annette fired back with a playful smile. "Your quiche was excellent, but the center of the crust was a little on the damp side."

"Touché," he held up his hands in surrender. "No one is perfect. As we've previously discussed, Tiger."

Annette narrowed her eyes in mock offense, but Gregory had a point. She knew her life was far from perfect. But for the moment, she couldn't think of a single reason why.

When Charlene made it home well after Tyler's bedtime, Annette was sitting in the living room with a steaming mug of chamomile tea and a baking show on the television.

She lifted her mug to her sister in greeting. "The kettle is still hot if you want some."

"Oh, thanks but no thanks," Charlene said. "I'd fall asleep before it could even steep. I'm exhausted."

Annette muted the television just as the host of the show was demonstrating what under-whipped and over-whipped egg whites looked like. "Does that mean you had a successful day out on the boat?"

Charlene flopped down on the end of the sofa and closed her eyes. "Before we get into that, how was Tyler?"

"Busy. Talkative. Wonderful." Annette shrugged. "The usual. I took him to dinner, and he ate a corndog."

"Big day," Charlene smiled. "Thanks for watching him."

Annette waved away the gratitude. "You know I don't mind. I love hanging out with him. Plus, it's good for you and Noah to get some alone time. How was it?"

"Noah caught fish; I caught a tan. Can't ask for more than that." Charlene peeked one eye open. "There was more than that, though."

"Intrigue. Carry on."

"Well," Charlene sighed, "Noah and I are dating."

Annette blinked at her sister. After a few seconds, she nodded slowly. "Yeah… I'm aware. You've been dating for months."

"We've been spending time together for months," Charlene corrected.

"Is there a difference?"

Annette had seen Noah around the house enough that she could almost believe they had a third roommate. He and Charlene spent all of their spare time together. Sometimes, Annette came home from work and found the two of them sitting in different rooms of the house, Noah reading case files and Charlene reading a book. They acted like an old married couple.

"Yes." Charlene sighed. "Well, no. Things will mostly be the same, but… it's a commitment. Noah's way of telling me he's committed to… well, we didn't get quite that far."

"Like courting?"

"What? No, it's… Okay, yeah. Yes, like courting," Charlene finally admitted. "It sounds old fashioned when you say it like that, but—"

"You're old fashioned," Annette shrugged. "So it fits. That's amazing, Charlene. I'm happy for you."

Charlene grinned. "Thanks. It's nice. And weird, too."

"Because of Davy?" It had been almost six years since Davy passed away, but after twenty years together, no one could expect Charlene to be over it. Annette didn't think it was possible to "get over" something like that. Frederick was still alive, but Annette knew firsthand how strange it was to be on your own after so many years married. It felt a bit like learning to walk again.

"I have to balance being happy I'm with Noah and missing Davy and wishing he was still here. I just have no idea how to do that."

Annette laid a hand on her sister's shoulder. "I think you're doing it right now. By being honest."

"I know, I know. It's just hard when it feels like all those years I spent with Davy—getting to know him, letting him get to know me, becoming comfortable with him—were for nothing. I know that's not true, but now that I'm doing it all over again with Noah… I don't know. I'm a little bitter, I guess. I'm supposed to be growing old and letting myself go." Charlene chuckled. "I'm supposed to start buying stretchy pants and cat sweaters because Davy and I would have been together so long that he wouldn't mind. But instead, I'm back in the dating pool."

"I know what you mean." Annette had thought Frederick was forever. She never imagined being separated from him. "Have you told Noah this? I'm sure he'd understand."

"I have. And he does," Charlene said. "He has been so great about everything. And with Tyler. He wants to be there for him."

"Of course he does. Tyler is amazing."

"He really is." Charlene smiled to herself. "Noah wants us to be a family, and I—" She stopped herself and suddenly grew serious. "I want to say something, but I don't want it to come off wrong."

"Say it."

"I don't want you to take this the wrong way because I don't mean it to—"

"Say it," Annette repeated. "I'll be fine."

Charlene sighed. "I just can't believe I'm this lucky. To have had Davy and Margaret. Even though things with Margaret were and are complicated. And then to have Tyler and Noah in my life now. And you, too. I'm amazed that I have had so many people in my life who I love and who love me."

There was a time when hearing Charlene wax poetic about her wonderful life would have sent Annette into a jealousy spiral. She'd spent the better part of her adulthood comparing herself to Charlene as if life was some kind of competition and Annette was always in the losing position. But confessing all of her old grudges to her sister and living with her for the last year had taught Annette that life most certainly was not a competition. Wishing someone else ill wouldn't make her problems go away; it would just make her bitter. Which is why it was so easy to be happy for her now.

"You aren't lucky, Charlene," Annette said. "You're worthy. You're an easy person to love, which is why so many wonderful people love you."

Charlene's eyes glistened, and she pulled Annette into a hug. "You're an easy person to love, too."

"Tell that to Frederick," she mumbled into her sister's shoulder.

"I don't have to. He came back for you."

"He came back for something," Annette clarified. "Who knows what it is?"

"It's you. I'm positive."

"He cheated on me for three years. You really think he just changed his mind and realized he actually wants to be with me?"

Charlene shrugged. "It happens. I mean… it sort of happened with us, didn't it?"

The reminder of their past stung. She and Charlene had come a long way towards repairing their relationship in the last year, but the five years Annette had spent avoiding her sister still hung heavy on her conscience.

"I'm no better than Frederick. Actually, no, I'm worse! I abandoned you after Davy died." Annette sagged. "I don't have a leg to stand on with him."

Charlene grabbed her shoulders and shook. "I didn't say that to make you feel bad! I'm sorry. All I was trying to say is relationships have ups and downs. People make mistakes and then apologize for them."

"Yeah, horrible people," Annette said, pointing at herself, "who need to make ginormous apologies."

Charlene chuckled. "And if you accept the ginormous apology, things might grow to be even better than they were before."

It was Annette's turn to pull Charlene in for a hug. "You're the smart sister. Did you know that?"

Charlene patted her back. "Obviously."

Lying in bed that night, Annette couldn't get the conversation out of her head. As much as she didn't want to admit she and Frederick could have anything in common, Charlene hadn't been far off. Annette had abandoned her sister because of her own insecurities and doubts, but they'd managed to mend their relationship. Now, they lived together and Annette got to know Tyler. So many great things had come into her life because they'd mended things.

Could Annette refuse Frederick the same chance she'd been given?

Plus, something Charlene had said stuck with her. Annette didn't want to feel like the last fifteen years of her life were a waste. She didn't want to have to start over with a new man and date all over again. Charlene had been forced to because Davy died, but Frederick was alive and desperate to get Annette back. It felt like she'd be stupid not to at least consider it.

Afraid of spending yet another sleepless night torn over what to do about Frederick, Annette grabbed her phone from the nightstand and dialed his number. It was the same number from when they were married. She'd had it memorized for years.

He answered after the first ring. "Hello?"

"Are you still in town?"

"Yes. I told you I'm not leaving until we come to a decision. And I haven't heard from you since our dinner."

"I've been thinking," she said.

"Thinking good things?" There was a smile in his voice. Annette could picture the hopeful raise in his eyebrows. The way he was probably biting the corner of his lip, nervously waiting for what she would say.

Good? Not necessarily. But she'd been thinking and it was time to do *something*. She and Frederick couldn't stay in this marriage stalemate forever. It was time to make a decision.

"I want to go get coffee tomorrow morning. We need to talk things through."

"Does that mean—"

"It means we can't move forward until we talk about this," she said. "*Really* talk about it. When we do, I think we'll both know what the next move is."

She heard Frederick exhale. "Coffee. Okay. Yeah, coffee. Let's do coffee."

"I'll text you a time and place," she said. "Goodnight, Frederick."

"Night, Annette. I love you."

She hung up without responding and rolled over. Exhausted, physically and emotionally, Annette closed her eyes and drifted into sleep. It wasn't the peaceful sleep she'd been hoping for, but it was better than nothing.

6

THE NEXT MORNING AT ANOTHER BROKEN EGG CAFE

"We could have met somewhere closer to your house," Frederick said. He tipped the pot of coffee in her direction, but she waved him away. "I wouldn't have minded the drive."

"I didn't mind, either."

He raised a brow. "Since when? You hate driving on the highway. Especially before you've had coffee."

"I had some at home when I woke up." At four A.M. But Annette decided not to mention that little detail.

She'd thought—naively, perhaps—that making a decision about Frederick would help her sleep better, but that was most decidedly not the case. She'd tossed and turned all night, slipping in and out of half-remembered dreams that left her feeling uneasy. When it was finally an appropriate hour to text Frederick, she sent him the address for a breakfast place in Mt. Pleasant. She'd never been to Another Broken Egg Café before, but she liked that it was in neutral territory. Sitting down with him on the island seemed like a step too far right now. Or a step too close, rather.

Frederick sat down the coffee pot and took a loud sip from his mug. "Interesting."

"What's interesting?"

He shrugged. "Just that you chose to drive here, you refused more coffee, and now you're eating pancakes."

Annette looked down at the brown sugar cinnamon pancakes in front of her. The golden syrup was warm and thick. It looked like a commercial. "What's wrong with pancakes?"

"They're your stress food."

She frowned. "No, they're not."

"You ate them the morning of our wedding, your first day teaching at Oakley, and every time you had to go to the dentist." He ticked off the list on his fingers and gave her a knowing look when he was done.

"Hm." Annette had never considered it, but maybe pancakes were her stress food. On any normal day, she preferred savory foods first thing in the morning. Annette would take eggs and sausage over a pastry any day of the week. Except today, apparently.

"Am I the reason you're stressed?" Frederick asked quietly.

Annette dropped her fork and leaned back in the green vinyl booth. Maybe they should have done a drive-thru breakfast so they could have this conversation in the car. The elderly couple sharing the morning paper across the aisle didn't look capable of hearing one another, let alone listening in on anyone else's conversations. But Annette still felt exposed.

"Obviously," she sighed. "You're the reason I've been stressed for a year. You threw our lives into a woodchipper, Frederick."

He dropped his head. "I know, I know. And I'm so sorry. That's why I'm here. To fix things."

"It's hard to imagine fixing this, isn't it?"

"Not for me," he said firmly. "I can imagine it perfectly."

Annette had tried to do just that, many times. But most of the scenarios she'd dreamed up in her head ended with her slamming the door in a crying Frederick's face. Not exactly the kind of happily-ever-after most people dreamed of.

"This feels like… like when I broke the handle off that mug we bought when we visited the U.S. Mint. Remember?"

"But I fixed that!" he said triumphantly.

She grimaced. "You superglued the handle back on. It looked fine, but coffee still dripped through the cracks whenever I tried to drink from it. My point is, not to get too metaphorical, is that I think we'll always have cracks."

He leaned halfway across the table and grabbed Annette's hand. Her instinct was to pull away, but she forced herself to stay. To look in his wide brown eyes and try. *Really try* to look at him the way she used to. Surely she owed him that much. No—surely she owed herself that much.

"But you and I aren't some old souvenir mug," he said.

"It's just a metaphor."

"I know it is, but it's still not right," he said. "Souvenir mugs are meant to be thrown away. We're more like a priceless family heirloom."

"Like my grandma's fancy dinnerware that we keep in plastic boxes in the basement? How special."

He huffed in frustration and then, suddenly, brightened. "We're like that pottery. What was it—Chinese, maybe? The bowls we saw at The British Museum in London. With the gold."

Annette knew exactly what he was talking about. It had been her favorite exhibit in the entire museum.

"Kintsugi. It's the Japanese art of repairing broken pottery with gold."

"Yes! Kintsugi. That's what we are," he said. "We may have cracks, but we can mend them with gold."

"I'm surprised you remember that."

Annette could visualize walking through the museum, hand in hand with Frederick. He'd seemed distant the entire trip, grumbling about the food she wanted to eat and the sights she wanted to see. He hadn't even wanted to go into the museum, but Annette had reserved their tickets ahead of time so he had no choice.

Usually, traveling was where they got along best. The excitement of new sights and sounds washed away the annoyances of everyday life. It was the reason they'd always prioritized taking trips together. But London was one of their last trips before Annette learned about his affair. No wonder Frederick had seemed disinterested in her.

"It was your favorite part of the trip. Of course I remember," he said. "Look, we can make it work. We can fix this. With gold, if you're up for it. I know I am."

"Maybe," she mumbled. "Maybe."

"Definitely," he said, sounding more certain than she'd ever heard before. "The fact that you're here means you want to try. Doesn't it? Otherwise, you would've kept avoiding me."

"You made it pretty hard to avoid you."

Frederick's mouth tipped into a half-smirk. It was the same devil-may-care smile that had drawn Annette to him in the first place. "You used to find my persistence endearing."

"Maybe I still do," she admitted. "Because you're right. I'm here because I want to try. Or, I want to try to try."

"Try to try?" he asked.

"It's not as easy as just forgiving you. You hurt me, Freddy." Annette's voice broke, and she took a steadying breath. She wasn't going to cry.

"You broke my heart. And you were the one person I never ever expected to hurt me. Ever."

"I know. And I'll never forgive myself for what I did to you. It should have never happened."

"Then why did it?"

Frederick looked at her, his eyebrows pinched in a kind of pained sincerity. "You'll hate this answer, but I really don't know. The only answer I can give you is that I wasn't thinking. About anything. Not about you or our life together or what it would mean if I was caught. I just... did it."

Annette huffed out a humorless laugh. "You're right. I do hate that answer."

"I've spent months and months trying to puzzle it out, and I don't have a good reason. I wish I could take it all back."

As much as Annette liked hearing that, it rang false. "You can't mean that."

"Yes, I can. Why wouldn't I?" he asked.

"Frederick, you have a baby." She said the words quietly. Like, if she whispered them, it would make them less true. Maybe they'd hurt less at a lower decibel. "You can't regret your child, no matter who you had to hurt in the process."

He shifted nervously in the booth. His fingers drummed against the handle of his coffee mug and then he pressed his palm flat to the table.

"It's okay," Annette said, even though she wasn't sure that was true. "I understand. I really do. Is it a boy or a girl?"

He shook his head. "That doesn't matter. I want to talk about us. Me and you."

"We aren't the only two people in this relationship anymore."

"Yes, we are. That has nothing to do with us. We can go back to the way things were. And all of that can be separate."

The idea was so ridiculous Annette almost laughed. "No, we can't. It's way too late for a return to normal, Frederick. You have a child. The entire dynamic of our relationship will be different. You have a responsibility to that baby now. Raising a child isn't something you can sneak around and do in secret. And I don't want you to. Hiding things is what got us here in the first place. I want us to be honest with—"

Suddenly, he reached out and grabbed her hand again. He gave her fingers a gentle squeeze. "I agree. I want us to be honest, too. So I'm going to be honest and tell you... I don't want to talk about the baby right now because I don't want to alienate you."

Annette blinked, unsure what to say. Frederick took the opportunity to continue.

"I want you to be clued into every part of my life—the good, the bad, the messy. But I'm afraid we won't stand a chance if we throw ourselves into the deep end before we learn to doggy paddle."

Annette chuckled softly. "These metaphors are starting to feel pointed. Are you making fun of me?"

"It seemed like the best way to get my point across," he said. "That teen lifeguard never expected a fully grown woman to not know how to swim. He thought you were just playing around, but—"

"I sank like a stone." Annette pressed a palm to her forehead. "I can't believe I let you convince me swimming was a human instinct. *'Everyone can doggy paddle, Annie. Just jump in.'* Idiot."

"In retrospect, there's probably a reason it's called the 'doggy paddle' and not the 'human paddle.' But when that lifeguard failed to perform their duties, who jumped in after you?"

Annette rolled her eyes. "You did."

Frederick smiled and then leaned in. "Let's start broadly and work our way up to the finer details. For now, can we just get to know each other again? I want to take things slow. I'm not in a rush. Because if things go well, I'm ready to spend the rest of forever making up for my mistake."

Doubts tickled at the back of her mind. But Frederick had a point. For now, maybe it was enough that they were having a pleasant conversation over coffee. They could sort through the details later.

She nodded. "Okay. Yeah. Let's get to know each other again."

"Good. Let's. Now," Frederick raised his hand in the air to call the waitress over, "can I order you some eggs and turkey sausage? Seeing you behind a plate of pancakes doesn't seem right."

Annette pushed the pancakes away. "Actually, yes. These are so sweet they're making my teeth hurt."

They drank too much coffee and ate breakfast until they were bursting. But more importantly, they talked. About everything and nothing. It was the kind of easy conversation Annette remembered from their marriage. Where one of them always had something to say, the conversation shifting easily back and forth. But at the end, it was difficult to remember what they'd actually talked about. It was a stream of consciousness shared between them; a kind of conversational ease built up over a lifetime. One that couldn't be squashed easily, it seemed.

At the end, Frederick paid the bill and walked Annette to her car.

"Can I meet you for lunch, too?" he asked.

"It's already eleven."

Frederick checked his watch. "Oh, look at that. Do you think Another Broken Egg has a lunch menu? Let's just head back in and—"

"I should go," Annette said through a smile. "Thanks for breakfast."

"No, thank *you*. For everything."

His eyes trailed slowly from her eyes to her lips, and Annette knew he was going to kiss her. She'd known him long enough to recognize the signs. But she didn't stop him.

Annette closed her eyes and leaned into the kiss. And when Frederick pulled away, beaming with obvious relief, Annette waved and got in her car....

Before Frederick could see the truth written on her face.

Annette had kissed her husband.

And she hadn't felt a single thing.

7

ONE WEEK LATER—SULLIVAN'S ISLAND ELEMENTARY SCHOOL

Annette jabbed at the ancient coffee pot in the staff lounge and mumbled under her breath. "Come on. Make one more pot, you old geezer. Don't die on me now."

The staff lounge at SIES had by far the worst coffee machine of any of the schools Annette worked at. Usually, she avoided the temperamental machine at all costs. But after an explosive episode with one of her more developmentally delayed students led to a formal intervention from the principal and a call to their parents, Annette needed caffeine.

"Give it up." Natalie strolled into the lounge and dropped into a blue plastic chair. "Maureen barely got Gunther to sputter to life this morning. She's usually the one with the magic touch, so if she can't do it, no one can. I think he's toast."

Natalie was a fifth-grade teacher and Annette's best friend. Her best work friend, at least.

Annette slapped the side of the pot like she'd kick a horse's hindquarters. "Gunther?"

"Yeah, like the coffee shop manager from *Friends*? Maureen actually said this pot has been around since before the show premiered. Happy accident."

"Was she joking?" Looking at the pot, Annette couldn't tell. It wasn't out of the question for it to be pushing three decades of service.

Natalie shrugged. "I can never tell with Maureen. Oh, and speaking of, she wants you to come pick up your flowers from the front office. She said they're messing with her allergies."

Annette spun around, coffee pot momentarily forgotten. "What flowers?"

"You didn't know? It's a big bouquet. Peonies." Natalie sighed dreamily. "They're my favorite. Which is why you'll have to forgive me for checking the card that came with them. I wanted to triple check they weren't for me."

"They were for me?"

"It was announced over the intercom an hour ago."

"Oh. I was dealing with a situation."

Natalie winced. "I heard about that. Sorry, I should have warned you. Kyler was having a hard day today."

"It's okay. It happens." All too often in Annette's line of work. Working with kiddos with developmental and speech delays meant looking for constructive ways to help them express themselves and their frustration. A lot of times, Annette could help Kyler release his frustration without a tantrum. But today was one of the few times where she had to call in outside forces for help.

Natalie nodded. "Well, I just saw the flowers and, unfortunately, they weren't for me. They were for you. From someone named Frederick."

Two bouquets in as many weeks. Annette had only received flowers from Frederick a handful of times during their marriage, so this was novel.

All of it was novel, actually. They'd been going on dinner dates most evenings when Annette got off of work. Frederick called her every night from his hotel room in Mt. Pleasant. He was working remotely while he tried to win her back, and he had a lot of free time on his hands.

"You know him?" Natalie prodded.

"You could say that. He's my husband."

Natalie raised a brow. "Excuse me? Since when are you married?"

"Since fifteen years ago."

"Leave Gunther alone and come explain." Natalie patted the seat next to her.

"I'd love to, but I need this coffee. Especially if I'm going to talk about Frederick." Gunther's power light flickered on for a moment, giving Annette a shot of hope. Then it flickered right back out. She groaned.

"Fine. You come sit and explain; I'll beat Gunther into submission." Natalie and Annette switched places, and she started fidgeting with the power cord and button mashing the power button with vigor. She looked over her shoulder. "So, let's hear it. Who is Frederick?"

"My husband," Annette said. "We were married for fifteen years. Well, we still are married. But we're separated. He cheated."

Natalie hissed. "Ah. Hence the flowers. So this is recent, then?"

"No, actually. We've been separated for the last year."

"Which explains why you never mentioned him to me." Natalie pulled out the power cord and blew into the light socket like it was an old video game cartridge. Annette didn't see how that would help, but she didn't want to interfere with the process.

"He cheated on me for the last three years of our marriage. I didn't like talking about it."

"Understandable. I'm so sorry, Annette. That's awful."

"It was. It is," she said. "But we've been... dating, I guess? I don't know what to call it. He left her and wants me back. He says he made a mistake, and he seems sincere."

"Smart man. Well, you know what I mean. A smart man wouldn't have cheated in the first place. But at least he's smart enough to realize his mistake."

Annette smiled. "Thanks. You're sweet."

"Are you going to take him back?" Natalie asked. "Before you answer, you should see the bouquet. It really is gorgeous. Looks expensive."

"I don't know what to think. I trusted him, and he cheated on me. I'm not sure if we can come back from that."

"I get it. I really do. I mean, I wasn't married—yet—but my fiancé left me at the altar. Like, literally. *At the altar.* We were up there in front of our families and the preacher and our friends, and he changed his mind and left."

Annette pressed a hand to her heart. "Oh my gosh. That's horrible, Natalie."

"Yeah, but better that than fifteen years into a marriage, right? Not to make you feel worse about things." She winced. "I'm not very good at Girl Chat. I'm sorry. I'm just trying to say that I understand what it means to be hurt. And I don't think there is a right answer. If Andrew had come back to me the next day and said he'd made a mistake, I probably would have taken him back."

"And now?" Annette asked.

"Definitely not. I'm in a different place now. Plus, I have my eye on someone else." She smiled sheepishly. "But it's all about timing. Maybe you needed a year away from Frederick to heal and process and now you two can get back together. Or maybe your time is passed and it's time to move on. There's no right answer."

Annette bobbed her head. "I guess you're right. But God, I wish there was."

"Don't we all," Natalie laughed. Suddenly, there was a horrifying gurgling sound from the coffee pot and Natalie threw up both hands in celebration. "Gunther lives to brew another day! It's a miracle."

"Bless you."

"You're welcome. But we shouldn't count on this miracle again. When you go get your flowers, be sure to sweet talk Maureen. Then I'll drop in later and compliment the picture of her chubby grandbaby on her desk. Maybe between the relief in her allergies and the high of talking about her grandkids, she'll be in a good mood and we can ask her to order a new coffee pot."

Annette laughed. "Now *that* would be a miracle."

Natalie shrugged and waved on her way out the door. "Stranger things have happened."

Afternoon At Annette's House

Charlene let out a wolf whistle when Annette walked through the front door. "That is a capital-B Bouquet! I thought the one delivered to the house earlier was nice, but this is a whole new level."

Annette struggled to see around the heavy peony heads in front of her. The pale pink blooms looked and smelled incredible, but after lugging them all the way home, Annette was tempted to dump them in the yard. "Wait, what? There's another bouquet?"

"It came an hour ago." Charlene pointed to the kitchen island. "I love lilies."

A bouquet only slightly smaller than the one in Annette's hands sat on the granite countertop. Red and blush pink roses were nestled amongst beautiful lilies of the same color. It was prettier than Annette's bridal bouquet had been. Frederick must have spent a fortune.

"Frederick still trying to get in touch?" Charlene asked.

Annette dropped her laptop bag on the floor and set the peony bouquet next to the lilies. "Well, actually, I've been meaning to talk to you."

"Uh-oh."

"No, not uh-oh. Everything is fine. I just haven't been completely honest with you."

"You're seeing him again?" Charlene guessed.

Annette twisted her lips nervously. "Yeah. How did you know?"

"You've been gone almost every night this week. I assumed something was going on. Plus, I heard you talking to him the other night on the phone. Don't worry," she added hastily, "I put in my ear plugs."

Annette and Frederick hadn't discussed anything earplug-worthy. Frederick still didn't want to talk about anything more serious than work and where they'd go for dinner the next day. They were taking things *very* slow on that front.

"Why didn't you say anything?"

Charlene shrugged. "It wasn't my business."

Annette sat down at the dining room table. Charlene had tile samples and paint swatches spread across the table in front of her. She was working on her latest flip house, a small corner property over on Waterway Boulevard, and was deep in the decorating phase.

"I'm sorry I didn't tell you. I'm barely sure I'm making the right decision as it is. If things go south, I didn't want to be even more embarrassed than I already am."

"What's there to be embarrassed about?" Charlene picked up a gray-flecked tile square and set it to the side with a cool gray paint swatch. Then she folded her hands in front of her, full attention on Annette. "Especially around me. I already told you, I'll support you no matter what."

"Yeah, but people stay stuff like that all the time. They don't always mean it."

Like, 'I'll love you forever,' or 'You're the only one for me.' Annette had been on the other side of those lies, and she didn't enjoy it.

"I meant it," Charlene said firmly. "All I care about is that you are happy. If Frederick makes you happy—and he is treating you with the respect you deserve—then I'm happy. Simple as that."

Annette looked at the bouquets blocking her view of most of the kitchen. "I think I'm happy."

"You don't sound confident."

"Because I'm not." Annette chuckled bitterly. "I'm not confident about anything. I used to be. You know, I never once imagined getting a divorce. Not because our marriage was perfect, but because... well, I didn't think anything could be bad enough that we couldn't work through it."

Charlene lifted one shoulder in a shrug. "And maybe you were right. Frederick wants to work through it now. Do you?"

Annette took a deep breath. This was the question that had been keeping her awake the last week. After her chronic lack of sleep, Annette was surprised she hadn't collapsed in a heap of exhaustion yet.

"I want to want to work through it. Does that count?"

"I'm not even sure it makes sense," Charlene laughed. "But whatever you want is fine. There are no rules here, Annette."

Annette groaned. What she wouldn't give for a guidebook. "The other day when you were talking about Noah—about how you sometimes feel like all the time you spent with Davy was a waste since he's gone now…"

Charlene winced. "Wow. That sounds harsh when you say it like that. I didn't mean—"

"I know what you meant," Annette interrupted. "Really, I do. And I completely get it. Because if Frederick and I don't work things out, I'm afraid I'm going to feel like the last fifteen years were a waste. You didn't have a choice with Davy because he is gone, but Frederick is still here… If we can make it work, then don't I owe it to myself to try to make the last fifteen years mean something?"

"Your life will mean something regardless," Charlene said. "Whether you and Frederick work out or not, the time you spent with him won't be a waste. But I see what you mean. And so long as you love him and want to be with him, and he loves and wants to be with you, then I don't see any reason at all why you shouldn't try."

Annette didn't realize how much she needed to hear someone say that to her until Charlene said it. Her throat tightened, and she swallowed down the emotion. "Then that's what I'm going to do. I'm going to try."

Charlene squeezed Annette's arm. "And I'm going to support you. No matter what."

She smiled at her sister and then tipped her head towards the bouquets on the island. "Do you want to support me by taking care of these flowers? If I touch them anymore than I already have, I'm pretty sure they're going to dry up and die."

"I forgot about your black thumb," Charlene cackled. "Yes, leave the flower tending to me. I'll take care of them."

Annette pressed a kiss to the top of Charlene's head before heading upstairs. "Thanks, Char. You're the best."

"And don't you forget it!"

～

A Few Days Later At Front Beachtro

Annette had the day off. Sort of.

It was an in-service day for teachers, but because she floated from school to school without a formal office, she decided to work from home. Or, in the case of today, from a charming little bistro near Front Beach.

It was mid-morning and relatively slow, so in place of the hostess who usually stood by the front doors of Front Beachtro, there was a chalkboard sign. *"Please seat yourself"* was written across it in a loopy cursive script. Annette chose a spot on the wooden bench along the side wall with the kitchen door in sight.

When the door swung open and Gregory walked towards her, smiling, Annette couldn't decide if her stomach dropped with excitement or dread. His red hair was freshly cut, and with the sides cropped short, Annette could see a bit of white and gray speckling around his temples. It suited him. "Dignified" was the word that came to mind.

"There you are. I was getting worried you weren't going to come back," Gregory said, handing her a menu.

Annette didn't even open it. "You can't get rid of me that easily," she teased. "I've just been busy. But today is a work-from-home day."

"And this feels like home? I'm honored," he teased right back.

Hardly. Annette didn't usually get sweaty palms at home. "Well, I don't have delicious scones and cappuccinos in my kitchen. Actually, now that I think about it, I'd rather live here."

"Ah, but you could have those things at home if you wanted."

"Does Front Beachtro do home delivery now?" Annette asked in surprise.

"Even better," he said, wagging his eyebrows. "I'll teach you myself. You said you wanted cooking lessons, right?"

"And you wanted help with your soggy bottom," Annette reminded him.

Gregory chuckled. "Exactly. So let's set the date."

Her heart started in her chest. *Yes! Yes.* She wanted to, of course she did. But she couldn't. Or could she? As she'd learned from Natalie and Charlene, there were unfortunately no rules for the situation she was in.

"Oh. Well, I'd love to, but I'm—I'm not sure if I—"

"Let's set *the* date," Gregory said with special emphasis. "It isn't a date. I know things are… complicated for you."

Her face flushed. Were her thoughts that obvious to read?

"Thanks for clarifying, but I'm mostly worried about my schedule," she lied.

Gregory nodded seriously, but there was a glimmer of amusement in his eyes. "Well, is your schedule full tomorrow? We could meet at my house for a lesson in the afternoon and eat the fruit of our labors for dinner."

She and Frederick hadn't discussed it, but it had become an unspoken rule that they would eat dinner together every night. If Annette suddenly canceled, she'd have to explain what she was doing instead. And she couldn't imagine talking to Frederick about Gregory.

Even now, Annette half-expected to turn around and see Frederick standing at the door watching her. That's part of the reason she'd avoided the bistro for the last week. Did it count as trying to save her marriage if she was making heart eyes at a red-haired restaurateur?

But this wasn't a date. And there was a difference between finding someone attractive and cheating. Annette wouldn't have separated from Frederick if he'd just found another woman attractive. He'd acted on it. And Annette never would never do something like that. Plus, Gregory was going to teach her how to make delicious scones at home. Once she could do that, she wouldn't need to visit Front Beachtro ever again.

Because the food was the only reason she was there. Just the food. Nothing else.

"I can make tomorrow afternoon work," she said.

"I'll write down my address and leave it on your receipt." Gregory backed away towards the kitchen.

"You never took my order," Annette reminded him.

He flashed a white smile. "You want your regular, right? Chef's choice?"

She smiled back. "You know me well."

Gregory really did know her well. He sent out her actual perfect meal: a skillet of cheesy scrambled eggs over oven-roasted potatoes, Italian sausage on the side, and a sriracha aioli.

Frederick who? While she ate, no one in the world existed except Gregory and his amazing breakfast skillets.

It was only when she finished that Annette realized fully how bad an idea it was to spend time alone with Gregory. Taking cooking lessons from someone whose personality and food made her weak in the knees was not a recipe for repairing her marriage.

But no matter how hard she tried, Annette couldn't bring herself to cancel. Instead, she tucked the receipt with Gregory's phone number and address into her purse and hurried out of Front Beachtro. Maybe, if she moved fast enough, she could outrun her guilt.

8

THE NEXT DAY AT GREGORY'S HOUSE

Annette sat in her car with her phone against her ear, hoping Frederick wouldn't answer.

She'd spent the day with Tyler, digging trenches and moats at the beach before going for ice cream. Frederick knew she'd be busy all day, and he hadn't asked to see her. Annette had a firm boundary around Tyler. She didn't want him getting attached if this thing with her and Frederick wasn't really going to work. Thankfully, Frederick understood.

But now, it was late afternoon, nearing dinnertime. He'd be expecting to make dinner plans soon.

"Hey, Annie!" He answered almost immediately, his voice chipper. "I know you don't care for it, but I really liked the Indian place we went to a couple weeks ago. And since I had seafood for the fourth day in a row last night, I feel like you owe me."

How anyone could be born and raised in South Carolina and not like seafood, Annette had no idea. Where Frederick was concerned, she'd given up trying to figure it out.

"Hi, Frederick."

"Don't sound so put out. Indian cuisine is more than just curry. I promise not to judge if you eat a whole plate of samosas," he said. "And we'll go out for dessert wherever you want to afterward."

She shouldn't have called. This was a conversation for text, and one wrong wiggle in her voice could bring the whole house of cards tumbling down.

On the other hand, there was nothing for Frederick to suspect, right? Gregory had made it clear this wasn't a date. That he understood she was in a complicated situation. There was nothing to hide, nothing to fear—and nothing that Frederick needed to know about.

"I'm not put out about that. I'd love to go get Indian food with you." She hesitated. She was laying it on too thick. "Okay, maybe not 'love,' but I would go get Indian food with you, but—"

"Oh no. Are you canceling?"

"I'm rain-checking," she corrected. "I... signed up for a cooking class."

Only a small white lie. Hardly consequential, in the big scheme of things.

"Oh." He paused. "Wait, really?"

"Yeah. It seemed, uh... fun."

"You hate cooking. I can count on two hands the number of from-scratch meals you made when we were together."

"That's an exaggeration."

"Whenever we had pizza delivered, you'd say, 'This is my specialty.'"

Okay, so he had a point. Eating food had always been an interest of Annette's, but cooking was a relatively recent hobby.

"I guess I haven't really had the budget to eat out every day like we used to." *Before you cheated* hung in the air, unspoken but ever-present.

Annette cleared her throat. "I had to make some changes to support myself on a teacher's salary."

The line went silent. Both of them stewed in the reality that they'd been apart for over a year. Their dinner conversations the last couple weeks were still polite and non-specific. Even the night Annette had stayed with Frederick in the hotel, the most they discussed was the state of their mortgage and whether Annette still wanted to be on his company's medical insurance. They talked around their separation the way they'd tip-toe around a bull in the center of the room—carefully, to avoid the horns.

"If you needed something, you could have asked." His voice was smaller suddenly, guilty. Which only made Annette's guilt ten times worse.

"I didn't need anything. I swear," she said as earnestly as she could. "But I like cooking now. I met the chef of a new bistro and he offered to teach me some tricks. It's really not a big deal."

If that was true, why was there a rock in her stomach? Annette shoved the question away.

"Okay," Frederick finally said. "It does sound fun. Maybe next time we can take a class together. Like a date."

The thought of Gregory teaching her and Frederick how to cook a romantic meal made Annette want to roll into a ball. Never, *ever* going to happen.

"Yeah, maybe," she said. "But I should probably get going. I'm about to be late."

"You're there already?"

Annette checked the address Gregory had scrawled on her receipt the day before against the silver numbers affixed to the siding of the house in front of her. "Yeah, I'm here."

"Then I won't keep you," Frederick said. "Have fun and call me when it's over, okay?"

"Okay. Bye."

There was a moment's hesitation before he added quietly, "I love you."

It was so quiet Annette could have missed it. That's probably what Frederick assumed happened when Annette hung up the phone without responding.

She silenced her phone and climbed out of her car. She really was running a little late. Only a few minutes, but still.

The house was a cheery yellow, raised up on stilts like every other house in the neighborhood to help protect against flooding. The garage under the porch was open, and Annette could see a white Jeep and a bright red golf cart inside along with a few bikes hanging from the ceiling. Did he ride, too? And why were there two bikes? Annette was trying to get a closer snoop—when she heard the front screen door slam shut.

"Welcome, welcome," Gregory stood behind the wooden railing and smiled. "You ready to get started?"

He looked great. Freshly showered, radiating a pleasant cologne, with a white button-down shirt rolled up to the elbow to expose brawny forearms.

Annette's heart jumped in her chest. This was a bad idea.

But she found herself nodding eagerly. "Definitely."

"What did those scallions ever do to you?" Gregory asked.

Annette blinked, resurfacing from deep inside her own thoughts. There was a neat pile of minced greenery in front of her that she had no memory of chopping. "I'm mincing them like you said."

Gregory reached over and pointed to the grooves in the cutting board. "Yeah, but we're liable to get wood chips in the meal if you don't ease up there."

"Oh." She winced. "Sorry. I was distracted."

"I can tell. Just relax." He shook out his arms. "Let the knife flow through the food. I just sharpened it, so you don't need to go all Incredible Hulk on those poor vegetables."

Now that he pointed it out, Annette could feel the tension across her shoulders. When she loosened her hand, her knuckles actually cracked. Okay, maybe she was a little tense.

"I'll try."

But a few minutes later, Gregory reached across the island and laid a hand over hers. "You're taking out your frustration on the cutting board again."

Annette groaned. "I'm sorry."

"This isn't an actual cooking class. You aren't being graded." Gregory gave her an encouraging smile, which only made the knot in her stomach tighten.

She liked that smile a little too much.

Really, it was that smile that had her lost in her head, anyway. Gregory had given her a quick tour of the main living spaces in his house. His decorating was all clean lines and warm colors, just like Front Beachtro's dining area. Clearly, he'd had a hand in designing both spaces.

Then they'd gone into the kitchen. "We're making caramelized onion and scallion scones," he'd said, grinning proudly as he presented his shiny white kitchen loaded down with the necessary ingredients.

And immediately, Annette had been weighed down by guilt. She'd told herself before she wouldn't have been angry at Frederick if he'd found another woman attractive. But what if he'd found them attractive and then spent time alone with them? Was this wrong? Was it cheating? Annette didn't even think she and Frederick were together just yet, so it couldn't be cheating.

Or could it?

From that point on, the lesson was a lost cause. Annette was hopelessly distracted by her own guilt. The only reason she didn't burn the onions was because Gregory guided her through every step of the process, including how to turn the stove top on.

"Are you okay, Annette?" Gregory pushed the cutting board out of the way and made her look at him. "If you don't want to be here, I won't be offended. We can call this off."

"What? No. I'm fine. I want to be here."

He raised one brow. "I'm not entirely sure you *are* here. You've been a bit... absent."

Annette sagged forward. "I'm sorry. It's just—well, things are—"

"Complicated?" Gregory finished. He gave Annette a sympathetic smile. "I don't know exactly what's going on, but if you need to leave to take care of something or if you want to reschedule, that's fine. I shouldn't have pressured you into coming in the first place. I'm sorry if you felt—"

"I'm dating my husband."

Gregory froze for a second. Then his mouth snapped shut. "I'm sorry?"

She sighed. "I told you my husband and I were separated, and I guess we still are. But he is in town, and we've been dating. I guess. I don't know. It's all complicated." Annette laughed, though nothing was especially funny in the moment. "How many times can I use that word, right? But that's what things are—complicated."

"Annette, this isn't a date," Gregory said gently. "I said that at the bistro. You're great, but we're just here to cook."

Annette could feel her face flushing. "I know! And you didn't give any other impression. I guess I just feel like maybe I owe you the truth of why I've been so absent today. Mentally, that is. I don't want you to think I'm not grateful for what you're doing. Or that I'm having a bad time or something. I'm not. This is—you are—great. My life is just—"

Gregory raised his eyebrows and grinned.

"—*perplexing*," she said, changing course at the last moment. "My life is perplexing."

"Nice save."

"Thank you."

Gregory wiped his hands on the dish towel over his shoulder and leaned back against the granite countertop. "So you're dating your husband? Frederick, was it?"

Annette nodded. "But we don't need to talk about this. Or him."

"I'm fine with it if you are," he said. "Especially if it means you'll stop mortally wounding my favorite cutting board."

The cutting board was a large rectangle of butcher block. Way nicer than the sheet of plastic Charlene had in her kitchen. The letters G.D. were carved in the bottom corner.

"Your initials?" she guessed.

"My ex-wife bought it for me."

Annette stiffened and then immediately tried to play it off. "Oh, that's —what a nice gift. Thoughtful. It's pretty."

Gregory chuckled. "Yeah, Laurel was a great gift-giver. One of her strengths. Definitely not one of mine."

"Mine, either," Annette admitted. "I once gave Frederick a fruit subscription for Christmas. We received a box of fresh fruit every month for a year. He doesn't even like fruit."

"Sounds like me! For our first anniversary, I gave Laurel a tool set."

Annette wrinkled her nose. "Why?"

"Because she was always asking me to do things around the house for her."

"Oh no."

"Yeah," Gregory laughed. "I thought maybe it was because all of the tools were mine and she didn't have any of her own. So I got her a set with pink handles and tried to teach her how to use them. Weirdly enough, she didn't appreciate the gesture."

"Gee, I can't imagine why!"

They both laughed and when the room went silent, Gregory leaned forward. "All I'm saying is, I understand complicated, too."

Looking up into his kind face, framed with silky auburn waves, Annette wished desperately that things weren't complicated.

"Frederick cheated on me," she spat out before she could stop herself.

"Oh."

"Yeah." Part of her wanted to slap a hand over her mouth and keep her messiness bottled up. But another part of her, a bigger part, felt like laying it all out there.

"He cheated on me for three years. And had a baby with the other woman. I don't know whether it's a boy or a girl yet. He won't say. He and I tried to have a baby, but it didn't happen. But now he has a baby with her. And now he left her and is in town to try to win me back."

Gregory's eyes widened at the onslaught. "*Oh.*"

Annette groaned. "Sorry. I shouldn't have unloaded on you. But we were being honest, and I—I'm sorry."

"Don't be. Really. It's fine. But I didn't all expect that."

"Believe me, neither did I," she drawled.

"And after all that, you're dating again?"

Annette couldn't even look into his eyes as she nodded.

"That sounded judgmental, but I didn't mean it to," he said. "I just want to understand where you're at right now."

"I get it. I never would have imagined even considering taking Frederick back after everything. But... being alone is hard." Annette felt her throat tighten. She cleared it, determined not to make this moment any more mortifying than it already had been. "And we were together for so long. Fifteen years. I don't want to throw that all away."

"That makes sense. If Laurel had wanted to give us another shot in the first year or two after we divorced, I would have given it a go."

"And now?" Annette asked.

"Definitely not. She's remarried now. And I'm the monogamous type." He winced. "That sounded like a jab at your ex, but I didn't—"

"It's fine." Annette waved him away. "Intended or not, Frederick deserves the jab. I mean, he cheated on me for three years."

"Fool." Gregory smiled at her over the island. Despite her having just dropped a lifetime worth of personal baggage on him, he looked remarkably unphased.

Annette took a deep breath and picked up the knife again. "Okay. I'm ready to focus up and learn. No more distractions. Definitely no more complications."

Gregory dumped the bowl of wet scone dough onto the floured countertop. "Sounds good to me."

She finished mincing the scallions and then helped fold the herbs, caramelized onions, and a generous pile of grated cheese into the batter. Then she shaped the mound into a disc and cut it into eight parts.

Gregory slid the baking sheet into the oven and closed the door with his hip. "Those will bake for about thirty-five minutes. When they come out, we'll brush them with more butter and feast."

At the mention of food, Annette's stomach growled. "I can't wait. I'm starving."

"Do you want me to make you something in the meantime? I'll admit, my fridge is a little bare, but I could whip up a sandwich. Or," he skidded over to his pantry door and pulled out an oily brown paper bag, "I tried my hand at homemade chips last night. For the bistro. They are greasy and probably stale. But if you're hungry, you can have them."

"Thank you, but I can wait."

"Did I undersell the chips?" he asked. "I feel like I undersold them. They aren't *that* greasy and stale."

She laughed. "You adequately sold them. But now that I have scones on the brain, nothing else will satisfy."

Gregory wiped his floury hands on the front of his apron and dropped down into a leather-covered bar stool. "Then we wait."

"We wait," Annette agreed.

They fell into a slightly awkward silence. Without something to keep their hands busy, there wasn't as much to talk about.

"Do you do a lot of experimenting for the bistro menu?" she asked.

"Only when I have the free time."

"And when do you have free time?"

"Every night of the week." He laughed. "I was hoping you wouldn't ask. It makes me sound pathetic."

Annette shook her head. "I don't think so. It means you have a job you love. Most people would kill for that."

"You said you're a speech therapist, right? Do you love your job?"

"Sometimes yes. Sometimes no," she admitted. "But I like being a teacher way more than I liked working at a bank. I'd rather deal with people all day long than numbers."

"I don't blame you for that. Without my business manager, my finances would be a wreck. That's one part of owning a restaurant I don't love at all—the money."

"Money is the main reason most people bother to work at all."

He ran a hand through his air, leaving a little dusting of flour on the front curls. "I like earning the money, but I don't like counting it or writing the checks. It's stressful. I'd rather let someone else deal with that so I can focus on the food."

"Have you always loved to cook?"

"Not even a little bit," Gregory laughed. "Until I met Laurel, I was the classic bachelor. It was all frozen pizzas and boxed pastas and jarred sauces. But once we got together, I started reading cookbooks and food magazines. I clipped out recipes."

"Wow. A regular Martha Stewart."

"If that's a compliment, then I accept heartily."

"I'd never dare insult my guru," Annette teased. "Especially when you were putting in the work to better yourself. It's admirable."

"Thank you. But it wasn't just for me. After all, you can't expect kids to grow properly eating junk."

Annette's eyes widened. "But you said… The other day you said you didn't have any—"

"I don't," he rushed to explain. "They were Laurel's kids, from her first marriage. Not mine. Well, not biologically mine, anyway."

Annette couldn't help it. She sighed in relief. Not because she'd care if Gregory had kids, but because she'd care if he lied about them. "Did you help raise them?"

He shook his head. "Barely. They were already teenagers when I met them. And I only saw them a couple weekends per month. They lived with their dad during the school year. Nice guy, actually. We went golfing a few times."

"That explains the golf cart I saw in the garage on my way in."

"Hardly," he laughed. "I'm terrible. The golf cart was left behind by the previous owners. It was written into the contract when I bought the house. Care for a ride?"

Taking a cruise around the island at sunset in a golf cart would definitely take this cooking lesson from platonic hangout to date territory. "Not with scones in the oven," Annette reminded him.

"Oh, right." Gregory glanced at the oven timer he'd set. "And that is exactly why I set timers. With no one to remind me, I lose track of what I'm doing."

"Martha Stewart didn't teach you to multitask?"

"She didn't teach me a lot of things," he smiled. "Like how to avoid soggy bottoms on my tarts."

"Where Martha Stewart failed you, Annette Campbell will pull through."

Gregory raised a brow. "Does that mean we'll be doing this again?"

Annette knew she should say no. If this experiment had taught her anything, it was that she was too socially stilted to spend so much time alone with a handsome man. However, it had also been an incredibly pleasant afternoon. Even including the spilling of guts. Maybe even especially because of the gut spilling.

"It's only right I return the favor," Annette said. "You helped me and now I'll give you some pastry tips."

"Still not a date, though."

"Definitely not," Annette agreed.

But later that night when Annette was sitting at the island in her kitchen, snacking on the last remaining scone from her lesson with Gregory, he texted.

Just wanted to make sure you made it home safe. I had a nice time today. Looking forward to our next lesson!

And try as Annette might, she couldn't shake the jittery, glowing feeling in her chest that it had been a date, after all.

9

EVENING AT ANNETTE'S HOUSE

"You called!" Frederick sounded genuinely surprised.

"I told you I'd call after my lesson." Admittedly, Annette had been home for a couple hours already. But she didn't think Frederick had any right to sound so shocked. She'd always been the dependable one in their relationship.

"Yeah, I know. It was just getting late."

"I always keep my promises." The words came out with more bite than Annette intended.

Frederick hesitated. "Yeah. I suppose you do."

The right thing to do would be to apologize, but Annette didn't have it in her. For some reason, she felt snippy tonight. Whether it had something to do with the unanswered text message from Gregory sitting in her inbox, she couldn't say. Or rather, she wouldn't say. Because Annette was fairly certain she knew the answer.

Weeks of "dating" her husband and going out to dinner every night had resulted in little more than an extra pound or two settling around her middle. She'd blame that on the pre-dinner breadsticks and chips and salsa. And on the post-dinner drinks. After all this time, they were supposed to be further along by now. Weren't they?

"What did you do tonight?" Annette changed the subject.

"Ordered a pizza. Watched a movie in my hotel room. Nothing much."

"You could have gone out."

"You were busy," he said.

"You could have gone out without me."

"I didn't want to."

What a turnaround. When they were married, Frederick was the one pushing for a night out. Annette was the one who was happy to watch a movie every night of the week.

"I don't like the idea of you shut up in a hotel room by yourself all day," Annette said. "You work from there, too. You need fresh air. To get out and see people."

"You make me sound pathetic. I get out plenty. Besides, you're the only person I know here."

"You could meet new people," she suggested.

"What for? I won't be staying here long, anyway."

Annette opened and closed her mouth. She hadn't spent a lot of time thinking about what would come next. If she and Frederick reconciled, would she have to move back to Asheville? She'd just reconnected with Charlene. And with Tyler. Would she have to move away from him? What about her job?

All of these questions sat on the end of her tongue, but they were heavy. Big topics meant for later, according to Frederick. But Annette didn't know if she could wait for later.

"When are you going to head back?"

Frederick seemed to realize what he'd hit on and backed off. "Oh. Oh, well... I'm not sure. Whenever I'm done here, I guess."

"And when will you be done here?"

He fumbled again, sputtering out something incomprehensible.

"Is it when I agree to take you back?" Annette pressed. "Or do you need to be back in the office before then? You can't work remotely forever."

"I haven't really thought about it." He was lying. Annette could tell. He was living out of a hotel room. It would be crazy if he wasn't thinking about when he could get back home to his own bed and his normal life.

"What about your child?" If they were going to do this, they might as well go all the way. It was time to discuss all of the big, off-limits things. "I'm sure you don't want to be away from them."

Frederick sighed. "We don't need to talk about this now."

"Yes, we do. We have to talk about it sometime. It's important," she said. "I don't even know if you have a son or a daughter."

He let out a long, slow breath. "A son."

Annette deflated. A son. Frederick had a son. With another woman. She'd thought getting answers would make her feel better.

"What's his name?"

"Jackson," he said softly. "Jackson Frederick Campbell."

If she hadn't already been lying down, Annette likely would have dropped to her knees. "He has your name."

"For now. Debbie has threatened to change it now that I've left," he said bitterly. "She isn't too happy."

"I can imagine." Annette really could imagine it. And as angry as she'd once been at Frederick and Debbie both, she had sympathy for the other woman now.

"She'll calm down, though. She always does," Frederick continued. "And when she does, you can meet him."

"Meet who? Jackson?" Annette knew who he was talking about, but it still caught her by surprise.

"Yeah. We're getting custody sorted out now, but when things calm down…"

Custody. Annette knew Frederick would want to see his child, obviously. But hearing it put like that, she realized how big a part Jackson would play in Frederick's life. It wouldn't be like babysitting from time to time. Frederick would be taking care of his son. Raising him.

"—live in Asheville," Frederick said. Annette had lost the thread of the conversation, so she scrambled to pick it up as he kept talking. "It makes sense because Debbie is there. And my mom. The further I move, the less time I get to see Jackson."

"You want us to move back there?"

He chuckled slightly. "I assumed. It's where our house is."

"I live on the Isle of Palms."

"You're crashing with your sister," he snapped. "That isn't your home."

"Neither is the house where you cheated on me." The words were out before Annette could stop them, but she didn't care. She meant it. "I can't go back there, Frederick. I can't live there like we did before. It would be playing pretend."

"But the house is almost paid off. Just a few more years and we won't have a mortgage. And we always talked about raising kids there.

That's why we chose it in the first place—for the school district and the big backyard."

"*Our* children."

"What?"

"We talked about raising *our* children there," she said. "Not *your* child."

"Jackson is *our* child," Frederick said softly. "Or at least, I hope he can be one day. You won't adopt him or anything since Debbie is in the picture. But you can be like a mother to him, Annie. Once you meet him, you'll love him as much as I do. I'm sure of it."

Chills ran down her arms and legs. Annette was surprised her phone was still pressed to her ear because her hand was entirely numb.

"We'll be co-parents with Debbie," Frederick continued. "Tyler will have a cousin to play with when we visit."

"I guess I… well, I never considered how often I'd have to see—" Annette swallowed. "How often I'd have to see Debbie."

She heard Frederick's breath hitch on the other end of the line. "She's Jackson's mom."

"I know," Annette hurried to say. "Obviously. You're going to be in Jacks—in his life, so you're going to be in her life. But I hated Debbie. And you, actually. For most of the last year, I didn't even want to think about her. And now I'm going to be a co-parent with her?"

Suddenly, Annette understood why Frederick had delayed this conversation for so long. It wasn't exactly a walk in the park. Hearing her new roles spread out before her—co-parent, stepmother—was a rude awakening.

"I'm sorry, Annie," he said softly. "I don't know what to say."

And what could he say? He'd apologized for cheating on her, but no matter how much they tried, they'd never be able to put it fully behind them. There would always be Debbie and Jackson. Now,

Annette had to decide if she could live with the constant reminders of her husband's infidelity. If she could help raise one of them.

"I'm sorry, but I'm feeling sick."

"Are you okay?" Frederick asked. "Do you need anything? I can come over if—"

"No!" Annette barked. She cleared her throat. "No, it's okay. Thanks, but—I must have eaten something bad. Food poisoning, I think."

Frederick winced. "From the cooking class?"

"Maybe," she lied. "I'm sorry, I... I have to go."

"Okay. Call if you need anything, Annie. I lo—"

She hung up and flopped back on the bed. Maybe it was karma for lying, but suddenly she did feel kind of nauseous. More likely, it was the bitter taste of reality. Because it certainly wasn't the onion and scallion scones. Those had been delicious.

Frederick wanted her to help him raise his child. Once upon a time, Annette couldn't think of anything better than having a baby with Frederick.

But not like this. No matter how much she wanted a baby, she couldn't help him raise the child he'd had while cheating on her.

Which meant Annette didn't have another choice. She had to end things with her husband.

～

The Next Day At The Beach

The sun beat down, making Annette's skin feel dry and toasted. She knew she should reapply sunscreen, but she didn't have the energy. She didn't have the energy for much of anything, actually. The only reason she was here at all was because Charlene had forced her out of the house.

"Isn't this nice?" Charlene smiled, leaning back on a beach towel. "A girls' day. We need to do this more often."

Their neighbor, Elaine, hummed in contented agreement. "Next time, I'll bring drinks."

"I have tea."

"Real drinks, honey," Elaine said. "*Adult* drinks."

"I could go for a drink," Annette said. "I think I need it."

"You need something," Charlene agreed. "Dad would've said, 'A slap upside the head.'"

Elaine patted Annette's arm. "Forgive your sister. She filled me in on your… situation."

Annette chuckled. "I didn't expect anything less."

"She tells me you're seeing your husband again?"

Annette mumbled noncommittally.

Charlene had been trying to drag details out of Annette since she'd found Annette sitting on the front porch in the middle of the night with a box of maple-flavored cream cookies. The package had been in the pantry since Annette had moved in a year earlier and she'd never opened them. But when life circumstances called for gross amounts of processed sugar, beggars couldn't be choosers.

"Annette is being vague," Charlene answered for her. "Something obviously happened, but she won't talk about it."

"Nothing happened," Annette lied.

"Liar!" Charlene leaned over Annette, blocking the sun and casting herself in silhouette. Ringed in light like that, she looked like an angel. A scary angel who liked to strong-arm people into admitting their deepest, darkest feelings. Charlene poked Annette's shoulder. "I didn't call Noah over to watch Tyler for nothing. Out with it."

"I never asked you to do that."

"She wouldn't even need to," Elaine said. "Noah loves that little boy like his own."

An uncomfortable feeling twisted in Annette's guts. Noah did love Tyler, deeply and truly. Annette knew she could never feel that way about Frederick's child. And she knew she and Frederick could no longer be together.

"There!" Charlene snapped and pointed at Annette's face. "That look in your eyes. What are you thinking about? You're hiding something."

Sweat was beginning to gather along Annette's collarbone and, even though she'd felt nauseous from the cookies all morning, she was suddenly ravenous. The only way Charlene was going to let her off the beach is if she spilled. So, if only to stave off the inquisition, Annette spilled.

"Frederick wants me to co-parent his little boy with him and Debbie, and I can't do it. So I have to leave him."

Charlene blinked a few times, stunned. Then: "A boy?"

"A boy," Annette confirmed. "Jackson Frederick Campbell."

"His name..." Charlene breathed. "I'm so sorry, Annette."

Her sister wrapped her in a hug, and Annette leaned in. Why hadn't she confessed all this the moment Charlene had found her two sleeves deep in the maple cookies? Telling the truth felt so much better than drowning in the lie.

"And I think I have a crush on the owner of Front Beachtro," Annette added. "His name is Gregory."

Elaine whistled. "I've seen him. What a looker! You have good taste."

"Good for you," Charlene clapped. "I'm happy you're moving on."

"I thought you wanted me to get back with Frederick."

"Me?" Charlene asked. "No. I told you I'd support you if you did."

"And now you want me to move on?"

"I'll support you if you do." Charlene tapped Annette's temple with her finger. "When are you going to get it into your head that I am only here to support you? All I want is for you to be happy."

"Me, too," Elaine added, raising her hand. "I want both of you girls to be so happy. You deserve it."

Annette felt tears prickle at the backs of her eyes. She wasn't usually so easily emotional, but she'd had a wild few weeks, so she cut herself some slack. "Thank you. Both of you."

"That's what we're here for," Charlene said. "So what do you think you'll do now?"

Annette groaned. "Call Frederick, I guess."

"That will be a fun conversation."

"Hah. Hardly." She laid back on the sand and stared up at the blue sky. "Do you want to call him for me, Char?"

"Fat chance."

"What about you, Elaine?" Annette teased. "Care to make a highly personal phone call for me?"

"I'm afraid not. I like to gossip, but I can't handle confrontation."

Annette sat up suddenly. "Do you think there will be a confrontation?"

"An emotional confrontation," Elaine clarified.

Charlene nodded. "Yeah. And if Frederick comes around the house like he did for Tyler's birthday, Noah will take care of him. Don't worry, Elaine. You'll be safe."

Annette wasn't afraid of Frederick. Not in the way they were thinking. She didn't think he would hurt her. But she was worried he'd try to talk her out of her decision. And Annette didn't know if she was ready for that just yet.

"And on the bright side, at least the two of you don't have a child together," Elaine said. "I'm a child of divorce, and watching my parents bicker and fight about custody and who got us for Easter and Christmas… it was a mess. But you and Frederick can have a clean break now."

Charlene shot Annette a sympathetic look. Apparently, Charlene told Elaine a lot of things, but she'd never told her how much Annette had wanted children. That she and Frederick had tried and tried for years with no luck. Annette appreciated that there were some things that stayed just between her and her sister. But that still didn't stop the comment from stinging.

Maybe kids would've saved this, though. Maybe kids would've stopped all this from happening in the first place.

Her stomach turned again—a familiar feeling the last few days. She might really be coming down with food poisoning or a stomach bug—although, in her experience, food poisoning didn't usually come and go in waves like this, or cause cravings between bouts that led the sufferer to shovel in an entire carton of old cookies.

Elaine was talking about her childhood, telling a story about the time she ran away for an entire day without her parents noticing because each of them thought she was at the other one's house.

But Annette wasn't paying attention. She was suddenly raking back over the last few days in her head.

Nauseous? Check.

Cravings? Check.

Emotional? Big check.

Period?

Annette sat up. Her ears were ringing so she couldn't hear what Elaine or Charlene were saying. She could barely see. The beach and ocean spread out before her, but everything felt flat. Two-dimensional. Annette had the sense that she could reach out and rip the world in half like a piece of paper. Was this a panic attack? She'd never had one, so she couldn't be sure.

For the first time since she'd gotten her period in eighth grade, Annette was late.

Her heart thundered. She reached up to lay a hand on her chest. To try and calm herself. But somewhere along the way, her hand changed course. Instead, it settled against the soft fabric that covered her stomach.

There might be a baby in there.

10

A FEW DAYS LATER AT WOMEN'S WELLNESS CENTER

The last time Annette had even seen a pregnancy test was when Grace Foley had taken one sophomore year of high school.

It was a few weeks after prom. Grace gathered Annette and a few other girls from fourth period Biology in the C hall bathroom for "moral support." After the toilet flushed, they huddled in the large handicap stall in the back corner, as if anyone coming in might not notice four sets of feet under the door. And they waited.

Later, it turned out Grace and her date, Ray, hadn't slept together at all. Grace only wanted everyone to think they had. But still, the memory stuck in Annette's mind all these years later.

The small cardboard box. The white plastic stick with the indicator window. Grace asking if they would be willing to babysit for her if the test was positive.

"I have no idea how I'm going to get my homework done," Grace had said, dropping her head into her hands while they'd waited.

The other girls had comforted Grace, but Annette had sat over Grace's test with an amused kind of wonder. She'd watched the little plastic window for ten minutes before the tiny blue negative finally appeared.

But Annette's home test was readable in under a minute. Two pink lines. Positive. Pregnant.

"Annette Campbell?" The nurse stood in the doorway with a clipboard and a light blue Carolina Panthers shirt tucked into her scrub bottoms.

Two different home pregnancy tests had been positive, but in Annette's mind, it wasn't true until a doctor confirmed it. So she'd booked an appointment with Women's Wellness Center as soon as possible. The office was stationed in Charleston, but one day per week the doctors came down to the Isle of Palms to see patients there. The only reason Annette got an appointment was because someone else cancelled. Lucky her.

The nurse led Annette to a scale and then into a small room.

"Did you leave a sample?" she asked. "At the other office, my desk is right next to the bathroom so I see everyone come and go. Here, I'm shoved in a closet in the back."

"I left one."

"Okay, good." The woman strapped a blood pressure cuff around Annette's arm and sighed as she stared up at the clock on the wall, counting along with Annette's heartbeat. Annette was certain her blood pressure would be through the roof. She'd been having a borderline panic attack for days. But after the cuff squeezed and released, the nurse unstrapped her. "Blood pressure is good. Mind if we run through family history?"

The questions were delivered in a monotonous script. Memorized years ago, probably. Annette barely registered them beyond a mumbled "uh-huh" or "no," while the nurse made notes on her chart.

Then the big one: "You're here to confirm a pregnancy, correct?"

"I am." Somewhere in the building, a nurse was dipping a stick into Annette's sample, waiting for the test to process. Annette should have asked a friend to come with her for support the way Grace Foley had.

"Great. The doctor will be by in a few minutes."

A few minutes later, the doctor walked through the door, a wide smile on her face. "Well, Miss Campbell, it's confirmed. You're pregnant. Congratulations."

Annette smiled and nodded. She was on autopilot. Her body knew what to do—be polite, look excited.

Inside, though, her mind whirled.

How had this happened? She knew *how* it had happened. But... how? After years and years of trying, nothing. But now... when they were mucking through the confused tangle of their lives. Why now?

Enough had happened in Annette's life that she knew there wasn't always a reason. Frederick had never given her a reason for why he cheated. Sometimes, life was as much blind chance as anything else. Dice gathered in a cup, shaken around, and rolled across the table.

With the doctor's confirmation, Annette knew how her dice had landed. But she still had no idea what game she was playing.

The conversation with the doctor passed in a blur. She left the office on her bike. Was it safe to still be riding a bike, considering the news? She didn't know, but she didn't have another option. Not unless she wanted to call Charlene and open up the entire can of worms.

As far as a destination, Annette didn't have one. She knew Charlene was at home with Tyler. There'd be no way for her to get inside and to her room without running into one or both of them, and she wasn't ready for that.

Front Beachtro was firmly off limits. Annette had already dumped enough of her secrets on Gregory without adding this whopper to the batch.

How she ended up at Elaine's house was anyone's guess. But as soon as Annette saw the older woman sipping tea on her front porch, a welcoming smile spread across her face, Annette knew she'd made the right choice.

"Shouldn't you be at work?" Elaine asked. "Or are you playing hooky?"

"I had a doctor's appointment. I took the afternoon off."

"Oh." A crease of concern formed between her wispy brows. "Everything is okay, I assume? Riding that bike every day the way you do, you must be fit as a fiddle."

"A pregnant fiddle."

Elaine's eyes widened at the same time as Annette's. The outburst had surprised them both.

"That's why I'm here, I guess," Annette continued. "I... I don't know what to do."

"Oh my." Elaine waved Annette up onto the porch and patted the cushioned chair next to her. "Sit down. Get off your feet. Should you even be riding a bike?"

Annette shrugged. "I've never been pregnant before."

"Me either," Elaine admitted. "It's probably fine. Besides, bigger fish to fry."

"Much bigger," Annette agreed.

"Is it—" Elaine cleared her throat. "I don't want to pry, but do you know... er, who is the baby's—"

"It's Frederick." Annette bailed Elaine out of the awkward interaction. "I thought maybe we'd work things through. Despite everything, I missed him. I was confused. Still am. And I... well, we—"

Elaine held up a hand to stop her. "What happens between a husband and wife is their business. You don't owe me an explanation."

"But is it his business?" Annette sagged, suddenly exhausted. "I mean, do I have to tell him?"

Technically, Frederick was still her husband. But what did she owe him? There was no rulebook for situations like this.

"It feels like perhaps you should. It might be a hard secret to keep," Elaine suggested.

"I was worried about telling him I want a divorce. Now, I have to tell him I'm pregnant *and* I want a divorce."

"You still want a divorce?"

Annette dropped her face in her hands. "I think so. Maybe not. I don't know."

"Okay, easier question: do you want some sweet tea?" Elaine asked. "I have a pitcher inside. I can go and get you a—"

Annette looked up at Elaine, tears brimming in her eyes. "What should I do?"

The woman's face cracked in sympathy. "Oh, honey. I can't tell you that."

"But you said the other day at the beach how horrible it was for you when your parents divorced. Surely you have an opinion."

"I'm not vain enough to think my opinion is the right answer," she said.

"Am I dumb to think having a baby could fix everything?"

"Well, I'm not sure I can—"

"Please," Annette begged, cutting her off.

Elaine turned towards her and sighed. "Are you keeping the baby?"

"Yes." That wasn't even a question. Annette hadn't considered another alternative for even a moment.

"Okay. Then, if you ask me, I think you have to tell him."

"Frederick?" Annette asked, though she knew who Elaine meant.

"He's the father. He deserves to know."

Annette's thoughts were like partially remembered lyrics from songs she'd once heard—they floated around her head in jumbled pieces she couldn't put together. But as soon as Elaine said it out loud, Annette knew she was right.

"I know he does," she said. "It would just be easier if he didn't need to be involved."

Elaine snorted. "Many things in life would be easier if men didn't need to be involved. Trust me, I know that as well as anyone."

"So I'll do it on my own. Charlene is doing it on her own."

"Hardly," Elaine said. "You're helping her. So is Noah. And I babysit. It takes a village, darling."

Annette groaned.

"Men are trouble, but they can be useful from time to time," Elaine said. "Even when they annoy the dickens out of you, you might miss them when they're gone. That's my experience, anyway."

"John was a good one," Annette said. She'd never really known Elaine's husband well, but the way Elaine talked about him, Annette knew he must have been a wonderful man.

"He was. But he made his fair share of mistakes, too. He never cheated on me, but, well… relationships are messy. And good people can make bad decisions." Elaine hesitated and then added quietly, "Do you think Frederick would be a good father?"

"Yes." Another question that was easy to answer. "That's part of the reason why I married him. I could picture a life with him. A family. I just never pictured it like… this."

Elaine rubbed Annette's shoulder but didn't say anything. She seemed to realize she'd already said enough.

"Thanks," Annette said. "I didn't mean to come here and dump this on you. You were just enjoying your day, and I—"

"Dropped by and made it even brighter," Elaine finished. "Seeing you is always a treat, honey. Always."

Tears clouded her vision. Annette laughed as she wiped them away. "My hormones are already out of control."

"Which is why you can always come talk to me about anything. Pregnancy and parenthood and life is hard enough. You shouldn't have to do it on your own. Matter of fact, I won't let you."

A Few Days Later At Charlene's House

Frederick stood in the entryway with his hands shoved deep in his pockets. "Charlene has done a lot with the place since I was last here. Nice woodwork on the stairs."

"She was prepping it to sell, but we're splitting the rent now, so..."

He nodded and looked around. "Is she here, or—?"

"She and Tyler are at Noah's house. We have the place to ourselves."

Delight flashed in his eyes. If only he knew why he was really there.

"I was wondering why you invited me over. I assume Charlene doesn't want me around?"

Annette gestured for Frederick to follow her into the living. "She doesn't care. She's supportive of whatever I want."

"Oh."

Considering the truth bomb she was about to drop, there was no reason not to be brutally honest from the jump. "Truthfully, Frederick, I didn't really want to bring you into my house. This is my space. If things weren't going to work out, I didn't want it tainted."

"Tainted. Ouch. Like I'm black mold." He dropped down onto the sofa and reclined casually, without a care in the world. "Does me being here now mean things are working out?"

"You being here now means we need to talk."

His smile disappeared, replaced with a furrowed brow. "What's going on?"

How many times over the years had Annette imagined this conversation? She'd considered buying him a present—maybe a small pair of baby shoes or a onesie emblazoned with *"I Love Daddy!"* Or she could take him out to dinner and tell him over food. It was their way, after all. Discussing big things over a meal.

But now, sitting across from her husband, still uncertain whether they should even be together at all, Annette decided simplicity would be best.

"I'm pregnant."

Frederick's face froze. The only thing that shifted was his eyes. They darted around the room like he expected to see cameras hanging in the corners. A film crew peeking through the window to make sure they were getting their shot.

"You're kidding," he said finally.

It wasn't even a question. He truly thought she was kidding.

"I'm not," Annette said. "I found out a few days ago."

He blinked. Annette waited. For all his confidence and bravado, Frederick always needed some time to process big news. Annette understood. She'd needed days to work up the courage to tell him at all.

Finally, he let out a ragged sigh. "You're serious?"

"I am. I started feeling nauseous and exhausted. My period was late. Then I ate these weird, stale cookies from the pantry and—"

"You've been to the doctor's office?"

She nodded. "They confirmed it."

He ran a hand around the back of his neck and squeezed. "I can't believe it. I mean... we tried for so long. *So long.*"

"I know."

He stretched back on the couch and stared up at the ceiling.

Before Frederick cheated, Annette thought she knew him as well as any person could know another person. When he fibbed and said he liked her oversized sweatshirt with the frilly shoulders, Annette could read the truth all over his face. When he ate her Thai leftovers and tried to deny it, she knew.

Until she didn't.

Suddenly, Frederick jumped up. There were tears in his eyes. "This is amazing, Annie."

It was Annette's turn to blink in stunned silence.

"It's finally happening." His voice cracked. "We're having a baby." Before Annette could stand up, Frederick dropped down to his knees in front of her. "I'm so, so happy."

Annette didn't need to be inside his head to know he was telling the truth. His hands were trembling on her back. Joy practically vibrated out of him. And this close—wrapped around one another in a way they hadn't been in years—the joy seemed to seep into Annette, too.

"I'm happy, too," she admitted. And she really was. Telling Frederick about the pregnancy had been so nerve-wracking that she hadn't stopped to consider how much she genuinely wanted this baby.

"This is the new start we needed," he said. "I want this with you, Annie. I've always wanted it. A family. A fresh start. You and me."

"Me, too." She held her husband as tight as he was holding her. "I want this, too."

11

EVENING AT FRONT BEACHTRO

Annette sat in the passenger seat of Frederick's rental car, arms plastered to her sides. If she wasn't afraid of making a scene, she would have locked the door and gripped the steering wheel for dear life.

"Let's go into Mt. Pleasant," she said. "That's where we usually go for dinner."

Frederick shook his head. "C'mon, Annie, I'm starved, we're here, it looks nice—what's the problem?"

"Or I can cook something."

"You've only had one cooking class," he teased. "You think you're ready for that?"

"Charlene can cook, then." Charlene wasn't even home, but Annette would call her back to the house if she needed to. Anything to get them away from Front Beachtro.

"Does your sister know you're pregnant?"

"No," Annette said. "But wouldn't that be a great way to tell her? We can share the news!"

She'd buy a billboard and put out an ad in the paper if it meant they didn't have to walk into Gregory's restaurant like this. Together. As a couple.

Frederick leaned over the center console and pressed a kiss to Annette's cheek. His next words were whispered in her ear. "I want it to just be the two of us tonight."

But it wouldn't be just the two of them. Gregory would be there. An unwitting third wheel, at least in Annette's mind. What kind of fresh start could she and Frederick really have if their first night out was to Front Beachtro?

Frederick climbed out of the car and walked around to open Annette's door. "Besides, I've heard a lot of people talking about this place."

"Who?" Annette asked. "I thought you didn't know anyone here."

"The concierge at the hotel mentioned it. And I've been doing a lot of restaurant research trying to find places for us to eat. Front Beachtro was top of my list for when you finally let me visit you at home. The menu looks great."

"It is, but—"

"I won't taint anything," he said quietly, wrapping an arm around her waist. "If that's what you're worried about. We're in this now, aren't we?"

Looking up into his eyes, Annette couldn't tell him she still wasn't sure. He was so happy, so filled with love for her and their future child. And Annette didn't want to let that go.

"Yeah. Yeah, we're in it," she said, leaning into him. "Let's go."

Walking through the front doors, Annette felt like she was the lead in a heist movie. Mission: enjoy a meal with her husband without being spotted by the chef.

"Two." Frederick said to the hostess and pulled Annette into him. She was unprepared and nearly toppled over. "Best table you have. We're celebrating."

"Oh, really? What are you celebrating?" It was probably part of the woman's training to feign interest in the guests. She didn't care why they were there. She just wanted to get through her shift and get home.

Frederick, however, was more than eager to share. "Can I tell her, honey?" The last time he'd smiled so wide was when Annette was walking down the aisle on their wedding day. She'd been sure he was going to pull a muscle in his cheeks. Fifteen years later, that was almost a certainty if he kept this up.

"It's just a fresh start, is all," Annette offered up instead. "We're toasting to new beginnings."

"That's lovely. Then I'll put in the order for some celebratory champagne," she said. "On the house."

Frederick tsked and reached over to lay a hand on Annette's stomach. "You better make those non-alcoholic."

The hostess's eyes widened in recognition as a pit opened in Annette's gut. She accepted the woman's whispered congratulations as graciously as she could, but she wanted to slide out of her chair and hide under the table.

Would their hostess go into the kitchen and tell Gregory? Was Gregory even working? Annette hadn't seen a sign of him since they'd arrived, but he was the owner, not waitstaff. On a busy night, he'd probably be back in the kitchen. And tonight was, by all accounts, a busy night. Two-thirds of the dining room was full with more people lining up along the sidewalk, eager to get inside.

Even if he was there, maybe they could blend in. If she just sat back, kept her head down, and made it through dinner, maybe no one else would pay them any mind.

"Free drinks. This place is amazing," Frederick said. "Maybe if I tell our waitress the news, we'll get dinner free."

"No!"

Frederick frowned. "I was just teasing."

"I know. I'm sorry." Annette shook her head. "It's just... it's early, you know? Anything could happen."

"You'll be fine, Annie. I know it. This wouldn't have happened if it wasn't meant to be."

She let out a bitter laugh. "Meant to be? I'm not sure I believe in that anymore."

"Well, I do," Frederick said. "I'll believe it for the both of us. You and I are meant to be. Always have been. And so is this baby."

"I hope you're right."

He kissed her temple. "I am. Things always work out in the end."

The waitress arrived with two fizzy concoctions. After confirming there was no alcohol, Annette tossed hers back. She wished she could have a real drink. She couldn't remember ever needing it more.

"Hey!" Frederick jabbed a finger at his menu. "Didn't you say you made scallion and onion scones at your cooking class? There are some on this menu."

"Oh. Yeah, I did."

Frederick looked at her, waiting for more of an explanation that Annette didn't want to give. It's why she'd been vague in the first place.

"Did I not tell you I took my class with the chef from here?" she asked.

"From Front Beachtro?"

She nodded. "Yeah. I come in her for breakfast and lunch sometimes. The owner is really nice. He offered to teach me a few things."

"That is *nice* of him." Frederick stared down at his menu, but Annette had the sense he wasn't really reading it. His eyes seemed to be fixated on one particular point.

Finally, he looked up. "He just opened this place up and is already offering cooking classes?"

"Apparently." Annette's eyes were boring their own hole in the dessert section of her menu. Maybe they could skip straight to dessert. Or better yet, leave a ginormous tip for the free drinks and get out of here. "I'm feeling nauseous. I think the food smells in here are making me sick."

"How many people were in the class?" Frederick asked, ignoring her. "The kitchen seems pretty small based on the size of the dining room. You must have been cramped."

"We weren't cramped at all," Annette said. "There was a lot of space. It was a private class. Did I not mention that?"

"No. No, you didn't."

"I didn't? I thought I did."

"Nope." His jaw flexed. Whatever joy there'd been from her announcement earlier, it was gone now.

"Huh. Well, I guess I'm telling you now: it was a private lesson. I should have saved a scone for you. They were great. But hey, we're at the restaurant. You can order one from the man himself."

"And who is the man himself, exactly?" he snapped.

"Gregory Dane."

Frederick ran his tongue over his teeth and nodded. His shoulders were tense. Try as he might to look relaxed, they kept shrugging up around his ears.

"He's very nice," Annette said. "I told him I was a helpless cook. He offered to give me a lesson, and I thought it could be nice. He was being nice."

"Nice," Frederick murmured. "I'm sure he was being nice. I'd be nice, too."

"What is that supposed to mean?"

He leaned back in his chair just as a waitress passed behind him. She had to swerve to avoid elbowing him in the head, and Frederick waved and smiled in apology. As soon as the waitress was gone, his smile vanished. "I wish you'd told me I was taking you to your boyfriend's restaurant for dinner."

"My boyf—Are you serious? Gregory isn't my boyfriend. I just told you that he asked me if I wanted to—"

"He asked you on a date," Frederick interrupted. "It was a date. You went on a date with him. And you lied to me about it."

"I told you I was taking the class!"

"You failed to mention it was a private lesson at his house."

"Because it wasn't worth mentioning."

He exhaled sharply. "So it was at his house?"

Annette opened and closed her mouth. Okay, maybe she'd been a little secretive about that part. "Yes. I already told you that."

"No, you didn't. I just guessed based on the way you're acting. You're a terrible liar."

"We can't all be as good as you," Annette mumbled. Hurt flashed in Frederick's eyes, and Annette regretted her words instantly. "I'm sorry. I shouldn't have said that."

Frederick held up a hand to dismiss her. "No. By all means, say what you mean. We're starting over, aren't we? Might as well be honest."

"We are starting over. Which means it isn't fair to hold things over your head," she said. "I'm sorry. I mean it. You've apologized, I accepted. So, I'm sorry."

All at once, the steam went out of the argument. Frederick gave her a sad smile. "To be fair, I have given you a lot to hold over my head."

"That's in the past. But we're moving forward."

"I hope so."

"Me, too." Annette slid her chair around so they were closer together. She grabbed his hand. "And while we're being honest, I didn't tell you about my cooking lesson with Gregory because I was confused. About you and me—where we stood. What I wanted. I didn't want to make things even more confusing by adding someone else into the equation. But nothing happened. It wasn't a date. He taught me to make scones, and I went home. That's it."

"Nothing else happened?" he asked nervously.

"Nothing else happened."

Frederick chuckled and ran a hand down his face. "Some celebration this is, huh?"

"It's fine."

"I wanted it to be a nice night. A night to remember. And now it's all…"

"Honestly, I've had more than my share of nights to remember," Annette said. "I'd love a night to forget."

"For most people that means get black out drunk, but considering your condition—"

Annette wrinkled her nose. "I'd love a boring night, is what I mean."

"A movie on the couch. With takeout. That way there are no dishes. Did I get it right?"

He smiled at Annette hopefully. And for the first time in way too long, Annette remembered why she liked being married. After Frederick cheated, everything had been colored. Whatever the opposite of rose-colored glasses was, that's what Annette had on for the last year. But there was an ease found in being with someone who knew who you were already. Someone who didn't need an explanation. Someone you didn't have to apologize to.

Annette had missed it.

"Yeah," she smiled. "You're right."

Frederick pulled out his wallet and tossed a twenty on the table. "Then let's get out of here."

He held out his hand, and Annette took it. She let him pull her to her feet. Then—

"Oh no! Are you two already leaving?"

Annette heard the voice and stiffened. She hadn't even seen him come out of the kitchen. The first time she'd lowered her guard all night and he'd snuck past her defenses.

Mission: failure.

12

EVENING AT FRONT BEACHTRO

She turned around and saw Gregory standing next to their table. Tonight, he had on the black button-down with the bistro's logo embroidered on the chest. He looked sharp.

"I think so," Frederick said, clueless. "We're a bit tired. But our waitress was lovely. That tip is for her."

Annette stared at Gregory, incapable of saying anything. All night, she'd been so worried about if he was at the restaurant and if he'd come out to see her that she'd never actually planned what to say if she did run into him. Now, here she stood, dumb and mute.

Gregory was eloquent, of course. And sane. He didn't have the same problem. "I just found out you were here. Madison told me. I thought I'd come out to say hi."

He was talking to Annette, but Frederick answered. "Wow. Nice service around here. Are we VIPs or something?"

If Annette was looking at Frederick, she'd know for sure whether he'd figured it out. Whether he knew he was talking to Gregory or not. But she couldn't seem to take her eyes off the bistro owner.

Frederick's hand was on the small of her back, two flutes full of some sparkling juice sat on the table, and Annette just wanted to explain everything to everyone. But she didn't know where to start.

Like everything else these days, it was complicated.

"Something like that." Gregory laughed easily. "Annette is a regular customer around here. And as a new business, I have to be nice to the regulars. I want everyone to feel like a VIP."

"That would make you Gregory, then?" Frederick stuck out his hand for a shake. "She's told me about you."

"Mostly about the scones." Annette finally found her voice. "They're delicious."

"She has raved about them. I'll have to try them the next time we're in. Because we really are tired." Frederick's hand on her back became firmer.

There would not be a next time. Annette would never bring Frederick here again.

"Of course. Our doors are always open. Except on Monday mornings. We're closed on Monday mornings." Gregory smiled. "I heard you were celebrating something, so I was planning to comp your meal. But we'll take a raincheck."

"How's Monday morning work for you?" It was a lame joke. Frederick's favorite kind. But Gregory laughed.

It was a fine conversation. Not the disaster Annette had imagined. Then Frederick carried on talking.

"A free meal—is that the customary gift for a couple expecting?"

Gregory's hands had been planted firmly on his hips, but they began to slide down until they hung limply at his sides. "Expecting? Like... pregnant?" He turned to Annette. "Are you pregnant?"

Annette couldn't breathe. It was like all the air had been sucked out of the room.

Frederick pulled her against his side and patted her hip. He was expecting her to answer. And the longer she went without responding, the worse the admission would be.

It felt a lot like skydiving. Frederick had convinced her it would be fun for their tenth anniversary. But Annette hated it. She was terrified of airplanes and scared of heights. She didn't even like riding in convertibles because of the wind. But as soon as they'd jumped out of the plane, there was no going back.

Right now, once again, she was freefalling with no other option—no other good option, anyway.

So she did the only thing she could do: she pulled the cord and nodded.

"Yes, I'm pregnant."

Time stretched like taffy, pulling and folding in on itself until Annette couldn't tell if it had been seconds or hours.

"Yep. We're having a baby," Frederick confirmed, shattering the moment.

Gregory blinked like he was just waking up. He looked at Annette, but she had the impression he was looking through her instead. "How far along?"

That single, innocent question was a Russian nesting doll—so many other important questions tucked away inside. He wanted to know how much she'd kept from him. Whether she'd known about this baby the entire time she'd known him. At the "cooking class," for instance. Did she know then? Just how complicated were things for her, after all?

"I just found out," she hurried to say. "A few days ago."

By design, Annette hadn't seen Gregory since learning the news. Until now. She'd avoided him because she hadn't been able to work out which would be worse: lying to him about the pregnancy or telling him about it. Now, she knew staying away had been the right call.

"Wow, that's—" He shook his head and smiled. "That's amazing. Congratulations!"

Is it? she wanted to ask. *Is it amazing?*

Frederick puffed out his chest. "Thank you. We're thrilled."

"And why wouldn't you be? A baby! You'll make great parents."

"Annie was born to be a mom. Plus, she's had a lot of practice."

Gregory frowned. "You mean because of Tyler?"

"Oh, yeah, I guess so," Frederick said. "But I was talking about me. She's been taking care of me for years."

Yet another bad joke that earned a pitying laugh from Gregory. Annette couldn't summon even that much. She felt nauseous.

Gregory seemed fine. He was smiling and congratulating them. Annette studied him for a sign that he was upset or jealous or anything other than bafflingly pleasant. But there was nothing. Just the same easy charm he always exuded.

Suddenly, Frederick's face was in front of hers. "Earth to Annie. Are you still with us?"

"What?" she blinked. "I'm sorry, I—"

"You spaced out."

Gregory's forehead was creased in concern. "Do you need some water or anything?"

"Yeah. I mean, no. I'm fine."

Neither Frederick nor Gregory looked completely convinced. "We should go," Frederick said. "Pregnancy is exhausting business." *As though he had any idea.* "But I hope you were serious about that raincheck, Chef. Because we'll be back for our free meal."

Not if Annette could help it.

"I never kid about free food. You are both welcome any time." Gregory smiled at Annette. "Any time at all."

Annette thought getting outside would help clear her head, but the humid evening air was stifling. It pressed in from all sides like a claustrophobic sauna.

"I'm sorry," Frederick said when they got into the car.

"Oh. About what?"

Blabbing their secret to Gregory?

Ruining her newly formed friendship?

Humiliating her?

"Gregory is really nice, like you said. I shouldn't have—what I mean to say is, I assumed the worst about you and him, and I'm sorry for that."

"Oh," she said again. "Well, thanks."

"He seemed really happy for you," Frederick remarked as he pulled away from the curb. "I'm not sure giving away free meals this soon after opening is a great business plan, but I won't turn it down."

"Happy" didn't seem like the right word for Gregory's reaction. But Annette couldn't quite put her finger on what the right word might be.

Frederick stretched his arm across the back of her seat and sighed. "Is it home for a forgettable evening then? I'll let you pick the movie we watch."

A forgettable evening? What a joke.

Annette would be replaying tonight in her head for a long, long time.

13

A FEW DAYS LATER AT FRONT BEACHTRO

How many times could you walk past a restaurant without having the police called on you for suspicious behavior? Annette knew she was pushing the limit.

But every time she passed the front doors again, she felt her skin crawl with anxiety. "Come on. Buck up, Annette," she muttered to herself.

An older woman strolled by just in time to catch the comment. She cast a worried glance in Annette's direction. In reply, Annette offered a friendly wave and tried not to look unhinged.

Forget the police—the men with big nets would be there any second if she didn't hurry and get off the sidewalk. So, with every ounce of courage she could muster, Annette propelled herself forward and opened the front door of Front Beachtro.

In her wild imagination, she'd pictured Gregory still standing next to the table where she'd last seen him. As if he'd been waiting there for her the last few days. But a chalkboard sign telling Annette to seat herself once again replaced the hostess. And, save for two women with strollers sitting at a table near the front window, the rest of the dining room was empty.

Neither woman looked up as Annette walked past and selected a table in the middle of the room. No lurking in the shadows this time. She wanted to be seen.

Charlene had advised her against going to the bistro at all. "I think it's inviting in drama. And stress," she said, casting a worried look at Annette's stomach. "The last thing you need right now is more stress."

"I'm not stressed."

Charlene gestured to the war zone their shared kitchen had become. Flour and powdered sugar dusted the countertops. The sink overflowed with baking pans and measuring cups and the island was stacked chest-high with baked goods Annette had made but couldn't bring herself to eat.

"This isn't because of stress. I'm... I'm trying out some new recipes."

"Looks like you're trying every recipe," Charlene snarked. "Just admit it: you bake when you're stressed. It's fine. You have good reason to be stressed."

"I'm not stressed!" Annette had slapped her hand down on the table, sending puffs of flour into the air. "I'm not stressed. I'm just... confused."

"About the baby?"

Annette shook her head. "I want the baby. No confusion there."

"So Frederick, then?" Charlene must have caught Annette's expression. "Okay. Not Frederick. Is it Gregory?"

"No. I don't know. Maybe?" She'd groaned. "I just don't like the way we left things. Frederick dropped the news on him. Last Gregory knew, things were 'complicated.' Then, suddenly, I'm rubbing my marriage and a baby in his face? I feel like I lied to him."

"But you didn't know about the baby the last time you saw him, did you?"

"No, but... I just think I'll feel better if I can explain myself."

"Will you feel good enough to get out of the kitchen?" Charlene asked. "Because I'll support just about any decision that means you get out of this kitchen so I can clean up. It's a state."

Annette had gone on to bake a batch of brownies and make a rough puff pastry. But before she could start on the custard filling, Charlene had physically forced her out of the kitchen.

"Baking is your stress reliever; cleaning is mine," she'd said. "Go forth and do what you must."

So now, sitting in the dining room of Front Beachtro, Annette was "doing what she must." Thankfully, she didn't have to wait long enough for doubts to creep in. A few seconds after she chose a table, the kitchen door swung open and Gregory walked out.

Annette sat up straighter. "Hi! How are—"

"I'll be with you in just a second," he said with a polite smile. Then he turned towards the women at the other table.

Annette listened as Gregory checked to make sure they were enjoying their food and complimented their chubby, fussy babies. He was as charming as ever. Which only made Annette feel even more insignificant. Gregory was this way with everyone. What they had wasn't special. It wasn't anything at all.

By the time he made his way back to her table, order pad at the ready, Annette was praying the big nets would scoop her up and carry her away.

"What can I get you today?" he asked without looking at her.

"Um, yeah, the usual."

"Remind me what that is?"

"Oh, uh, chef's choice. You haven't failed me yet." She tried to sound chipper. Normal. "But I actually came in to talk to you—"

"We had a call-in order that cancelled too late. They asked for the breakfast platter." He tucked the order pad in his back pocket. "Can I just give you that? It will get you in and out faster."

"I'm not in a rush."

He looked up and smiled, but it was a flat expression. The kind of dead-eyed smile Annette recognized from her staff badge for work. The receptionist at the superintendent's office hadn't done a countdown or given her any kind of warning before taking the picture, so really, Annette was lucky she had even that sad excuse for a smile. But seeing the same expression on Gregory, she didn't feel lucky at all.

"Right. Yeah. Hang out as long as you want," he said. "I'll be right back with your food."

Had their entire relationship before this moment been in Annette's imagination? It sure felt that way. Gregory was treating her worse than the women with the babies who'd only ordered one coffee each and a bowl of fruit to share.

Just as he said, Gregory came right back out with her food. The cast iron skillet sizzled, and Gregory slid it onto the table with an oven-mitted hand.

"Careful. It's hot."

"You don't say?" she teased. A wall of steam obscured his face slightly.

"Anything else I can get for you?"

Annette took a deep breath. "Well, actually, I came in to talk to you about the other night."

"Do you want this meal to be comped?" he asked.

"What?"

"The other night, I offered you a free meal," he explained. "I assumed your husband would be with you, but this is fine, too. Your baby, your choice."

"I didn't come for the free meal."

"I'll give it to you anyway," he said with a wave of his hand. "Your meal is on the house. Congratulations again."

"Thanks." It felt like the wrong thing to say, but every other possible response escaped her. "But I actually—"

Gregory snapped his fingers. "A drink. I never got you a drink. Coffee?"

"Yeah. Or no, actually. Water, please," she said. "But—"

"One water coming right up."

Before she could say anything else, Gregory whirled away and disappeared into the kitchen. When the door swung open a few minutes later, a pretty young waitress with a messy blonde bun came out carrying her water.

"A water for you," she said sweetly. "Do you want anything else?"

"No. This is all," she lied. "Thanks."

The breakfast platter was clearly meant to be a crowd pleaser. The flavors were basic. An all-American breakfast that anyone would enjoy. It certainly hadn't been hand-selected by a chef for her. Still, the scrambled eggs were fluffy, the ham slices were caramelized and tender, and the peppers and onions were soft but still had a nice bite. It was delicious, but Annette couldn't enjoy it.

Every time the kitchen door swung open, she turned towards it. She felt like one of Pavlov's dogs at the sadder tail end of the experiment.

Chatting and bantering with Gregory had become comfortable. It was pleasant. Annette was trained to expect his charm and attention. Now that she wasn't getting it, she was a drool-covered, pathetic mess.

The moms and their babies strolled out of the bistro a few minutes later. An elderly woman and her granddaughter replaced them. The same blonde waitress came out to take their order and deliver their food. Still no sign of Gregory.

"Can I get these plates out of your way?" the waitress asked.

Annette wanted to say no. Without the plates, she'd have no reason to stay. But what could she possibly want with dirty dishes?

"Sure," she relented. "Thank you."

"Anything else I can get you? A refill?"

She'd already had three. Anymore and she'd burst.

"No. Thank you. Just the check, please."

Maybe he'd come out to deliver the check. Congratulate her again, say goodbye, something at the very least. Then Annette could stop him and—

"I hear your meal is on the house today," the waitress said with a smile. "You're good to go."

Or maybe not.

"Oh. Right. Thank you."

Annette tried to sneak a peek into the kitchen when the waitress took her dirty skillet back, but the door swung shut too quickly. She hesitated for a few moments, waiting to see if it would swing open again.

It didn't.

She tossed a twenty on the table and left.

14

THAT EVENING ON THE BEACH

"Fancy running into you here." Elaine waved as she walked down the beach towards Annette. Her sandals dangled from her fingertips. "Mind if I sit?"

"Go ahead." Annette's voice came out raspy from disuse.

Charlene was too nervous to let Annette near the kitchen so soon after she'd cleaned it, so baking was off the table. Without her stress reliever—Fine! Charlene was right. She liked to bake when she was stressed—Annette didn't know what to do with herself. So, she'd planted her bum in the sand and hadn't moved in hours. Her legs were getting tingly from a lack of blood flow.

Elaine dropped down and sighed. "What brings you here today?"

"Charlene kicked me out of the house."

"She mentioned you've been baking a lot," Elaine said diplomatically. "She gave me a goody bag when I met up with her on our morning walk. The little cookies with the white stuff in them, the, oh goodness, what do you call—"

"Browned butter white chocolate chip cookies," Annette said.

Elaine whistled. "Yes, those. Those are delicious. A winner for sure."

"I'm glad someone could enjoy them." She pointed to her stomach. "Baby doesn't like sweets, I guess."

"So why bake at all then?"

"Charlene says it was stress-induced, but I just had a lot of energy."

"Oh yes, the very common burst of energy women feel immediately after finding out they're pregnant." Elaine laughed. "You're supposed to be resting, dear. Taking naps and relaxing."

Annette laid back on the sand and folded her hands over her still-flat stomach. It was bizarre to think there was a tiny human in there. Maybe once she had a bump it would be easier to believe, but Annette wasn't sure even that would do the trick. Pregnancy was strange.

"I have been resting. Sort of," she said. "I've just been... distracted. Dealing with some personal drama. I had a bit of a falling out with someone and—"

She snapped her attention to Annette. "You and Frederick?"

"Not Frederick," she said quickly. "I told him about the baby and everything went fine. He was excited."

"That's what Charlene said. She told me you two were working it out."

"Of course Charlene told you," Annette chuckled. "Do you two talk about everything?"

"Not everything." Elaine sounded slightly cryptic. But before Annette could question it, she moved on. "If Frederick took the news well, then what's the problem?"

"Really the problem might be that Frederick took the news a little too well. He wanted to go out to dinner to celebrate and he told the entire waitstaff about the pregnancy. Practically shouted it from a mountain top, actually."

Elaine laughed. "Sounds like he was excited."

"He was. He is," Annette said. "We both are. But... he made things sort of complicated for me. With a... friend."

"Which friend?"

"Gregory."

"Ah. The bistro owner. Handsome man," Elaine said with a devilish smile. "I've been in there a time or two. Good service. Great food."

"Yes, well, Frederick told Gregory about the baby."

"Is that so bad? He would have found out sooner or later."

"Right," Anette said. "But the news was kind of, I dunno... dumped on him all at once."

"Was he upset?"

"No. At least, I don't think so. Probably more surprised than anything else. And, I mean, I can't blame him for that," Annette said. "The last time we'd talked, I told him Frederick and I couldn't have kids."

Elaine's eyes widened. "Oh. So you two were good friends, then?"

"I guess so. Yeah. I mean, we were friendly."

"Very friendly, from what it sounds like. In my experience, men don't care much about your past unless they plan to be in your future, if you know what I mean."

"I know what you mean, but Gregory isn't like that. He's... nice," Annette said. "That's the only way to put it. He's a nice person. He's friendly to everyone."

"But he's mad at you right now?"

"He isn't even mad at me. Not outwardly, anyway. I feel like he's upset, but outwardly, he's just... normal."

Elaine frowned. "Hm. How so?"

"Well, take this for example: I went into the bistro today and he was nice to me. Perfectly nice. But something about it felt off. He was treating me like—he acted like I was just a normal customer."

"Aren't you?"

"Aren't I what?"

"Just a normal customer," Elaine suggested. "You met him at the bistro. You go there for meals. Sounds like a normal customer to me."

Annette blinked. "Well, when you put it like that, it sounds—it makes it sound like I just go there for food. But we're—he is my..." She thought about it for a few seconds and then grimaced. "What are you doing to me, Elaine?"

Elaine patted Annette's back. "Trying to get to the truth. Is it working?"

"Too well," Annette admitted. "I'm upset because Gregory treated me like a normal customer instead of someone he might be interested in. Which is crazy. Because I'm married and pregnant. Why should he treat me any differently than any other customer who walks into his restaurant?"

"He shouldn't."

"Exactly!" Annette sighed. "But I wish he would. How horrible does that make me? Oh gosh, I'm the worst."

"You are not the worst. You're going through a lot. And you're pregnant."

"That's no excuse."

"It is, though," Elaine said. "Your whole life is changing right now. You're allowed to freak out a little bit."

"But Gregory doesn't deserve to be on the receiving end of it all." Annette buried her face in her arms. "I just want to explain myself. Make sure he knows I didn't lie to him. I really didn't think Frederick and I could have kids. But now he probably thinks I'm some kind of psycho. Or a pathological liar."

"I very much doubt that, dear."

"For all he knows, I lied about Frederick and me being separated! I could have lied about not being able to get pregnant. Then I show up at his restaurant with my husband and announce that I'm pregnant. It's all so unhinged. No wonder he hid from me today."

"Wait, he hid from you?"

Annette nodded. "He took my order and then didn't come out of the kitchen again. He was clearly avoiding me. Didn't take a genius to put two and two together."

Elaine pursed her lips and hummed. "Maybe the problem is that you tried to talk to him there in particular."

"But that's where we've always talked."

"Exactly," Elaine said. "There, your dynamic is customer and restaurant owner. Maybe it was okay to chat and be friendly before, but now that you're with Frederick again, maybe Gregory doesn't know how to treat you. You said he's a nice guy. He's probably worried about overstepping his bounds."

That did sound a lot like Gregory. Under different circumstances, Annette would applaud a man for backing off once he knew a woman was taken. But in this case…

"I don't really know what the 'bounds' are anymore, you know?"

"Then you should talk to him and figure some out."

"I tried that! It was embarrassing. And too close to loitering for my liking." Annette wrinkled her nose.

"Meet somewhere else," Elaine advised. "He won't want to talk about this at his work. Pick somewhere neutral. Like the beach. Or a park."

Frederick had sent Annette flowers at work and that had felt uncomfortable. Why hadn't Annette considered hashing out personal business at Front Beachtro might feel weird for Gregory?

Annette turned to Elaine, one eyebrow raised. "Are you a psychologist?"

"I wish. The money would probably be better."

"You could definitely be a psychologist. Or a life coach."

Elaine laughed. "Please. I'm just a nosy old woman who always has to offer up her two cents."

Annette reached over and squeezed Elaine's hand. "Nose away. I'm grateful for any penny you can spare."

15

NEXT DAY AT THE BEACH

Was a picnic on the beach neutral? The idea had seemed harmless enough, but now that Annette and Gregory were sitting on opposite corners of a checkered flannel blanket with finger foods sitting between them, she wasn't so sure.

"I've never had a cheese log at the beach." Gregory scraped at the log with a cracker. Then he glanced at the carry out container of chicken alfredo Annette had brought along. "Or pasta."

Annette wrinkled her nose. "Is it weird? I think I might have let my cravings do the talking when I was at Harris Teeter."

"No, it's not—" Gregory laughed. "Okay, it's a little weird. But it's not bad."

"There's probably a reason you're the chef."

"Perhaps." Gregory smiled and leaned back on one arm. He didn't look like he was uncomfortable or having a bad time. But it was hard to tell with nice people. Maybe he just didn't want to hurt her feelings.

He wouldn't have agreed to come if he didn't want to. Annette had to keep staring out at the ocean and repeating those words to herself. She'd gone through them a hundred or so times and she still wasn't quite sure she believed them.

"So," he said, clapping his hands together to get rid of cracker dust, "this is nice. But I do have to wonder what prompted it."

"Prompted what?"

He waved his hands to the spread around them. "This isn't my usual Thursday lunch setup."

"What is your usual setup? Do you eat at the restaurant?"

"Sometimes," he said. "I also like to go home. It's good to get out of the kitchen from time to time."

"But you still have to make food when you go home, right? Or are you one of those people who leave their job at work? Like, you cook all day so you won't do it at home. Is your freezer stocked with microwavable dinners?"

"I'm offended at the insinuation," he joked. "I take pride in my palette. Really, Annette."

She laughed. "Sorry. So you take a break from the kitchen at work by going to your kitchen at home. Got it."

"I know that doesn't sound like a break, but it's like... like the difference between using the bathroom at work and using your bathroom at home. One is obviously better, right?"

Annette nodded. "Oh, yes. I mean, Tyler really needs to work on his aim, but that's still better than sharing a public restroom with four-hundred elementary students."

He winced. "Yikes."

"To put it mildly. Especially since I have to use the bathroom so much more..." *Now that I'm pregnant.* No matter where she steered the conversation, pregnancy kept popping back up. The plan had been to chit-chat and then ease into the pregnancy talk. But at this rate,

Annette would be laying herself bare before they even touched the alfredo.

"How are you feeling, by the way?" he asked, swallowing a large bite of cheese and cracker. "With the, uh, baby and all. How are things going?"

"Me? Fine. I'm fine. How are you?"

His brow rose. "I'm fine… How are you?"

"Fine."

Annette picked fuzz balls off of the flannel blanket and flicked them into the sand. She'd set up an umbrella for shade, but it was only shading the lower part of her legs now. Sweat gathered on her scalp and threatened to drip down her forehead, but she tried not to swipe at it. She didn't want to look nervous.

"Annette."

"Yeah?" she asked, not looking up.

"Annette," Gregory said again, softer this time.

The gentle tone took Annette off guard. She looked up to find him smiling. "What?"

"You can talk to me."

"We are talking." She knew she was being obtuse, but it was easier than being honest.

He pursed his lips. "*Really* talk. About your life. Your pregnancy. About Frederick."

She winced. Try as she might, the words just wouldn't come. They kept getting stuck behind the lump in her throat.

"Isn't that why you asked me to lunch?" he continued. "To talk about your big news?"

"I asked you to lunch because we're friends."

"Sure, and friends usually talk about their spouses and children. It would be weird if they didn't."

Annette sighed. "I know. You're right. It's all just... weird."

"Why is it weird?" he asked. "It doesn't have to be weird. Is it because of me? Am I making you uncomfortable? I'm not trying to."

How could Gregory be so nice? Annette was acting like a feral human who had never been socialized and he had the decency to ask if *he* was the problem. Unfathomable.

"No! Goodness, no, you didn't do anything," she said. "It's me."

"You're not weird."

"On the contrary, I'm acting like a crazy person," she said. "I'm not handling this—or anything in my life—particularly well."

Gregory sat up. "You aren't giving yourself enough credit. I think you're doing great."

"That's because you're a saint. If I was you, I'd stay so far away from me."

"I've been trying to," he said.

Annette froze. Her heart stuttered to a stop. "Oh. Okay."

"No, wait—"

"I shouldn't have asked," she said quickly. "You made it clear the other day that things have changed. And that's okay. It's my fault, anyway. I shouldn't have put you in the middle of my complicated situation."

"Annette, stop for a second," he said. "That came out wrong."

She stopped spiraling. Temporarily. Just long enough to see what he had to say.

"I just meant that I've been trying to keep my distance. I was probably acting weird when you came in yesterday, but I was trying to navigate this new situation. I didn't know quite where we stood, so I gave you space. Out of respect," he said.

Annette frowned. "Respect for me?"

He shrugged. "For you, for your relationship. You and Frederick came in for dinner and, I don't know… it kind of felt like a message."

"Oh my gosh. That was—that's why I'm here to talk to you," she said. "I'd just told Frederick the news. He wanted to celebrate."

"Yeah. I got that part."

"Right. I didn't want to talk about *that*." Annette took a deep breath and tried to compose herself. She hadn't felt composed since she'd taken the pregnancy test, but she had to try. "I want to talk about—I want to explain what happened. With the pregnancy. And Frederick."

"You don't owe me an explanation, Annette."

"I kind of do, though. I mean, last time we talked, things were 'complicated.' But what I dumped on you that night was more than complicated."

He chuckled. "It was a surprise, certainly."

"It was a surprise to me, too! I had no idea," she said. "I still can't believe it happened. I didn't think I could get pregnant. When I told Frederick, he wanted to celebrate. I was so frazzled I didn't even think about him taking me to your restaurant. Then when we got there, I couldn't think of a reason why we shouldn't go inside. Believe me, I tried."

"Oh."

"Yeah." She paused, wanting to leave it there. But what was the point of bringing Gregory all the way out to the beach with her weird assortment of grocery store foods if she wasn't going to be honest? "It kind of felt like maybe you and I… maybe we had a connection. Like if things became uncomplicated for me, maybe we would—"

"But things *are* complicated," Gregory interrupted, a little chill creeping into his voice. "That's why I tried to give you some space. Once I knew you and Frederick were—*are* together, I backed off. I didn't want to make you uncomfortable."

"I didn't want to make *you* uncomfortable!"

He smiled faintly. "Neither of us wanted to make each other uncomfortable. That's nice."

"I still don't, but I do want you to know that I was being honest the last time we talked. About everything. I didn't know I was pregnant then."

"I believe you."

"And I wasn't officially back with Frederick then, either." Annette's face burned with embarrassment, but she pushed through. "I wouldn't have led you on if I knew I was going to get back with Frederick."

Gregory reached over a laid a hand over hers, stilling her. "Hey, I believe you. Besides, it wasn't even a date, remember?"

His mouth was tipped up in a smirk. Annette couldn't help but smile, too. "Right."

"Just two friends casually hanging out. Learning to cook," he said. "It doesn't have to be more than that."

"Just friends."

He nodded. "Just friends."

Annette sighed in relief. "Okay. Well, that works out great then."

"I think so. I could always use more friends."

"You could? I can't imagine you not having enough friends."

He waved her away. "You can never have too many friends."

"I can," Annette said. "I'm more of a quality over quantity person. I'd rather have a few close friends than a lot of acquaintances."

Gregory grinned. "Does that make me a close friend?"

"Well, considering you're one of four people in my life who know I'm pregnant, I'd say we're pretty close."

"True. And you've offered to help me with my soggy bottom. That isn't something casual acquaintances do."

Annette tipped her head back and cackled. "This joke has officially gone too far. I may never eat pastry again. The mental image I now have is upsetting."

"I don't care if you eat it, but can you make it? Because you still owe me a pastry lesson." He wagged a finger at her. "I gave you the cooking lesson, so I expect my payment. Don't forget."

She held up one hand as though taking a solemn oath. "Never. I keep my promises."

"Good. I like that quality in a friend." Gregory winked and Annette felt light. Lighter than she had in weeks. Months. Maybe even in the last year.

"Okay," he continued, "now that we sorted that out, can I please convince you to come back to Front Beachtro with me and get a normal lunch? This spread you've created is—"

"Is what?" Annette challenge.

"Well, look at it," he said. "You know."

"No, I don't. But go ahead, don't be shy. Tell me what you really think. We are *friends*, after all."

"As your *friend*," Gregory said, "I have to be honest and say this spread is a culinary nightmare. It's like a bad Italian restaurant mixed with my aunt's Thanksgiving side dishes."

Annette fought back a laugh. "It's not that bad!"

"It's bad," he argued. "The cheese is hot and starting to melt. I think sand blew into the pasta. And orange juice? Really?"

"Maybe the orange juice was going a little too far."

"Way too far. If I have to eat this, I'll be the one who is nauseous." Gregory stood up and held out a hand. "Come with me. I'll make you and the baby a real meal."

Annette took his hand and let him help her to her feet. "Fine. But there better be scones involved."

~

There were scones.

So many scones Annette didn't know if she'd ever be able to eat again. She felt stuffed and bloated. Yet another beautiful symptom of pregnancy.

"Are you still in there?" Annette whispered, hand resting on her stomach. "Or did I squash you with carbs?"

The baby didn't feel real. The doctor had confirmed it and she had all the right symptoms, but Annette still couldn't imagine a tiny human in there.

"You probably don't even have ears yet, do you? Why am I even asking? It's not like you can answer. Or hear me." Annette chuckled at the absurdity of talking to her barely six-week-old baby. "But if you can hear me... I'm your mom."

Tears welled in her eyes, and she blinked them back. She'd already cried at a commercial for a genealogy testing service she saw on TV, and then again when Tyler split his chocolate chip cookie with her before bed. But she wouldn't cry again. Girl Scout's Honor: no more tears.

"The voice you heard earlier, that was Gregory. He's nice. He's... my friend." Annette smiled. "A good friend. You'll like him... if you ever meet him."

The news of the pregnancy had been such a shock that she and Frederick hadn't sat down to talk about their plans again. But she had to assume the baby didn't change anything. He still had Jackson. No matter what, he'd want to live closer to Asheville.

And Annette would have to go with him.

Frederick had a life in Asheville. His career. His friends. His child. She couldn't ask him to give all of that up.

"You'll have a good life. You'll have me and your dad. But you'll have Aunt Charlene, too," she said. "And your cousin, Tyler. He's a wild child, but you'll love him." More tears stung at the corners of her eyes —so much for her promise to herself. "Then there's Elaine. She lives down the street and is very wise. Maybe too wise. But she's the best. And like I said before... there's Gregory."

A full-on sob lodged in her throat, making it impossible to speak.

Saying it all out loud, Annette realized how much she'd be giving up. She'd built a life for herself on the island over the last year. Not just a temporary one, not a hollow sham of one, but an honest-to-goodness *life*. She didn't want to let it go.

Annette choked down her tears and rubbed her stomach again. "You're going to have a good life, little one. No matter what."

16

A FEW DAYS LATER—SULLIVAN'S ISLAND ELEMENTARY

Annette was sitting in the staff lounge, a ginger candy shoved under her tongue, when Natalie walked through the door.

"How goes it?" Natalie asked, moving immediately to the coffee station.

"It goes." First trimester nausea was so bad it was all Annette could do to sit upright. The urge to curl up in the fetal position on the threadbare gray-blue carpet was strong. But the baby was still a secret, so Annette swallowed her misery. "How goes it with you?"

"Fine." Natalie popped a coffee pod into the machine and pulled down the lever. "I could use something a lot stronger than this instant coffee garbage, though. You know, I'm almost starting to miss Gunther."

The old staff coffee pot had been in the lounge so long there was still a ring of rust on the counter where it had sat. The janitorial staff couldn't find a cleaner strong enough to clear it away. Someone had written "Gunther was here" next to it in permanent marker.

"Really? I never took you for a coffee snob."

"I'm not," Natalie said. "It's just that this burnt-tasting brown water is not coffee. It's dumpster juice."

The description made Annette's stomach turn. She sucked harder on her ginger candy. "You sound like a coffee snob to me."

Natalie grimaced into her mug and took a sip. "Okay, maybe slightly. I like to think of myself as a 'connoisseur.' And it's only because I almost married into a family that made coffee their business."

"The fiancé that left you at the altar?"

Natalie nodded. "His family owns a few coffee shops in Charleston. I think they're planning to expand, but I haven't seen anything about it online."

"You look him up online?"

"No." Natalie wagged a finger. "I do not look *him* up. I look the coffee chain up."

Annette chuckled. "Skating by on technicalities, I see."

"I have zero interest in reconnecting with him. But I'd do unspeakable things to have another one of their maple vanilla lattes."

"Can't you just go buy one?"

"Not unless I want to see my ex-almost-sisters-in-law. They all work the front counters." She sighed. "It's a tragedy."

"If the worst part of getting left at the altar was losing out on the delicious lattes, then I'd say you're doing okay."

Natalie cackled, but her good humor didn't last. As soon as she took another sip of coffee, she frowned. "Aside from the dire coffee situation here, how are you? I had a sub last week when you were here. We have a lot to catch up on."

Natalie had no idea exactly how much, and Annette couldn't tell her. After Frederick had dropped the baby bomb on most of Front

Beachtro, Annette made him swear he'd keep his mouth shut. So it wouldn't be fair for her to turn around and blab the news whenever she felt like it.

But just because she couldn't talk about the baby didn't mean she couldn't talk about everything else that was going on.

"I'm back with Frederick."

Natalie's eyes widened. "The ex-husband who sent the beautiful peonies?"

"Yes, that ex-husband. As opposed to my many other ex-husbands."

"Just trying to keep them all straight."

Annette snorted. "Well, Frederick and I worked it out."

"Did the flowers sway you?"

That and the accidental pregnancy, she drawled in her head. Out loud, she said, "Not as much as they swayed you."

"Peonies all day. White or blush," Natalie said decisively. "I'm a sucker for a good bouquet. Take notes. My birthday is in February."

"I'm a terrible gift giver, so I'll remember that." Then Annette realized with a jolt that she didn't have any idea where she'd be in February.

More and more, the topic of moving had come up. Frederick had actually been back in Asheville for a few days to talk with a lawyer about custody arrangements for Jackson.

"Can I tell him we'll be moving back to the area soon?" he'd asked before leaving. "It will make my case stronger. I'm arguing for fifty-fifty custody."

"Do you need to give them an answer right now? Can't it wait?"

"The sooner I let them know, the better. And what's the harm? Even if we don't have an exact date set, we'll be going back eventually."

Annette had nodded vaguely. Hummed some noncommittal response.

"Great," he'd said. "I'll be back in a few days."

Since then, they hadn't talked much beyond a few texts and one quick phone call. Part of it was that they were both busy. But Annette may have also lied about lesson planning late one evening to get out of talking to him. Because, frankly, she didn't know what she wanted to say.

Suddenly, Natalie's face was in front of hers. "Where did you go?"

"What?"

"You spaced out," she said. "Also, you look kind of pale. Are you okay?"

Annette's stomach was churning with either nerves or pregnancy nausea. These days, it could be either—or both.

"Yeah, I'm fine."

Natalie raised one eyebrow. "My lie detector is going off."

"Where can I get one of those?" Annette asked. "It would come in handy."

Natalie tapped her forehead. "It's built in. I'd share if I could. But why do you need it? Is it Frederick?"

"No. I mean, yes. He's definitely the reason I have trust issues. But I trust him right now."

"Just right now? As in, that could change?"

Annette hadn't really thought about it, but yeah. It was easy to trust Frederick when he was living out of a hotel in IOP, visiting her every single night, texting her all day. But what would happen if they moved back to Asheville? When he was in close contact with Debbie again?

"He wants to move back to Asheville. To be close to his son," Annette said. "And I guess—"

"You're moving?" Natalie pouted out her lower lip. "If I'd known that, I would have thrown that bouquet straight in the trash. Frederick who?"

"I know. I don't want to go. But... it's his son, you know?"

Natalie sighed. "Yeah, I guess. Sorry for interrupting. Continue."

"I'm just worried what our relationship will look like when we're back in the real world."

"Is this not the real world?" Natalie asked.

Annette shook her head. "Not for him. He's living in my world. He doesn't have his job here or his friends. He isn't going out for game nights with his buddies or for after-work drinks."

"Ahh, I gotcha," Natalie said. "There's no opportunity for him to cheat here."

Annette didn't like saying it so bluntly, but... "Exactly."

"That's hard."

"And it's not the only issue," Annette continued. "I'm also going to have to be a stepmom. To the child he had while he was cheating on me."

Natalie winced. "That's a big ask. It's not the kid's fault, but that doesn't make it any easier. Plus, you'll have to see the mom, too."

"I met her once," Annette said.

"No way! Before or after?"

"It was a few months before I found out. I picked Frederick up from work because his car was in the shop, and he was standing on the curb with her. They were just chatting, but something about the way she looked at him—when he got in the car, I told him I thought she had a crush on him."

Natalie gasped. "What did he say?"

"He laughed it off."

Uh-oh. Is somebody feeling jealous? were his exact words. She shivered at the memory. "I almost forgot about that. At that point, he'd been sleeping with her for years."

"Can you handle seeing her regularly? Or letting him see her regularly?"

"I could." And it was the truth. Annette could do it. She'd smile and be polite when they had to hand Jackson off. Even if she didn't like it. "The worst part might be everyone I won't be seeing regularly."

Natalie beamed. "Like me?"

"Like you," Annette smiled. "And my sister, my nephew, Noah, Gregory—"

"Gregory? Who's Gregory? Do I know Gregory?" Natalie was like a bloodhound on a scent. Annette could have sworn she saw her ears perk up.

"He owns a restaurant by Front Beach. Front Beachtro."

Natalie chuckled. "Like Front Bistro. I get it. Clever."

"He is," Annette said. "And the nicest guy."

"Is he handsome?"

Annette jerked to attention. "What? I don't—I mean, I guess. But I don't see what that has to do with anything."

Natalie pointed at the top of her head. "It has to do with me being single and in search of a nice guy. Preferably one that won't no-show on our wedding day."

"Oh, well... yeah, he's good-looking." It felt like Annette had to drag the words out of her throat. She wanted to lie. *He's hideous. A sweaty troll. Look elsewhere, you won't be interested.*

But why would she lie? Gregory was her friend. Natalie was her friend. It would be nice if her friends dated...

Right?

"Maybe Gregory can be your parting gift to me," Natalie said. "You can introduce me before you leave forever."

Natalie was being playful, but the words hollowed Annette out.

When she left, Gregory's life would go on. He'd make new friends. Maybe meet someone special. Someone like Natalie. Annette should be happy at the thought. She wanted Gregory to be happy. So why did she feel like she was going to be sick just thinking about it?

"I'm not leaving forever."

"Oh, right," Natalie said. "You'll come back for visits. Your sister lives here, so I'll see you again."

"No." Annette shook her head. "I mean... I don't think I'm going to leave."

"What?"

"I don't want to move away," Annette said. "I want to stay."

Natalie's eyes widened. "Have you told Frederick that?"

Annette took a deep breath. "Not yet. But I will."

17

LATER THAT NIGHT AT ANNETTE'S HOUSE

Frederick sat across from Annette at the dining room table, drumming his fingers on the wood while Annette ate.

"Sorry I already ate," he said for the third time. "I didn't realize you were cooking."

"It's okay," she mumbled around a large bite of food. "I should have called you."

Truthfully, Annette hadn't planned to cook at all, but the craving for breakfast burritos had hit her like a Mack truck. Now, she was shoving a sausage and egg burrito in her mouth so she wouldn't have to find the words to talk to him.

"Your dinner smells better than the hamburger I had," he said. "But last night, I ate at Port Plato."

Annette whimpered. "I haven't been there in ages."

"Since our anniversary two years ago," he said. "We split the chicken chimichanga."

"And you ordered those donuts in the berries and cream sauce."

"Which you ate entirely by yourself!" he laughed. "I'm still bitter about that."

"You should be. They were delicious."

The night in question, they'd gone to dinner at Port Plato and then walked to a three-story used bookstore down the block. Annette wandered around for an hour, and Frederick didn't complain once. He trailed behind her, smiling whenever she looked back at him. He'd seemed happy just to be with her.

Six months later, she was on the Isle of Palms and he was with Debbie.

Annette took another large bite and stared down at her plate. It was almost empty. She'd have to talk to him soon. *Really* talk to him. And she wasn't ready.

"I wish you could have been with me," he said. "Maybe I should have waited until we could have gone back together, but I was celebrating."

"You said on the phone the meeting went well."

He nodded. "It went so well. Better than I expected, actually. The lawyer doesn't see any reason why Debbie and I won't split custody evenly."

"You told him you'll be living in Asheville?"

"Yeah. And that you and our child would be with us, too. He liked the idea that Jackson would have a sibling. That's another thing working in my favor."

Guilt twisted in Annette's stomach. "What would it look like if you weren't in Asheville?"

Frederick shrugged dismissively. "Weekends, if I was lucky. Probably every other weekend. Maybe less. Depends on the mood of the judge, at the end of the day."

Annette ate the last bit of burrito, chewing slowly to earn a few extra seconds. Since her conversation with Natalie that morning, she knew what she wanted to do. But that didn't make it easier to say.

Before Annette could even finish chewing, Frederick stood up and grabbed her plate. "Are you done with this? I'll put it away."

She watched him rinse the plate in the sink and slide it into the dishwasher. Charlene would be annoyed that he put it where the cereal bowls are supposed to go. Then again, she was annoyed when anyone aside from her touched the dishwasher. The woman had a rigid organizational system.

"Well, what next?" Frederick stretched his lower back. "I could go for a walk."

"A walk! Yes." Annette practically jumped out of her chair. This conversation would be better had on the move. "A walk sounds nice."

He chuckled at her enthusiasm. "Apparently."

Annette changed into sandals and Frederick took his loafers off when they reached the sand. He set them next to the path that led back up to Charlene's house and then held out his hand. Annette didn't see a reason not to take it. She loved Frederick. Despite everything, that had never changed.

"I'll miss being so close to the water," he murmured. It was early evening, but the sun was already setting. The sky was awash in pastels and a breeze tossed Frederick's hair across his forehead. It was longer than he usually kept it, closer to the length he'd worn it in college. "We'll have to find lots of excuses to come back and stay with your sister. She'll have the space in that big old house. Do you think she'll get another roommate?"

Annette chewed on her bottom lip. "Probably not."

"Hm. Can she afford that place by herself? You did say she has two flip houses going right now. Business must be good. Or do you think she and her boyfriend will move in together?"

"I'm not sure, honestly." Annette hadn't thought about any of that. But things with Charlene and Noah were getting serious. Moving in together was the next obvious step, especially since Noah practically lived there already.

Suddenly, Frederick stopped, pulling Annette to a stop with him. "You're quiet tonight."

"Am I?"

He raised a brow.

"Sorry," she said. "I guess I—I've been thinking."

"Uh-oh."

She gave him a sad smile. "I've been thinking, and I'm not so sure I want to move back to Asheville."

He blinked and it felt like hours passed in those few seconds. His face was perfectly flat, expressionless.

Finally, a crease formed between his brows. "You don't want to move back home?"

"That's just it: Asheville isn't home for me. Not anymore."

"It's only been a year since you left," he argued.

"Yeah, but it's been a big year, don't you think?" Frederick didn't say anything, so she continued. "I learned how to live on my own here. I found a job I love. And friends. I have a life here, and I'm not so sure I'm ready to go back to the way things were."

He stepped forward and grabbed her other hand. "It wouldn't be the way it was before. I made a mistake and—"

"I don't mean Debbie. I mean… Don't you remember how quiet our house was in the evenings?" she asked. "I'd be watching a movie in the living room and you'd be in the den. Or maybe we'd both be in the living room, but you'd have your headphones in, watching some documentary. It was always quiet. Like we didn't have anything to say to each other."

Annette hadn't thought much about it then, but she couldn't imagine going back to the silence now. It would be like living in a mausoleum.

"That was then. Things can be different."

"Maybe," Annette said. "But I'm not sure I can take that risk. Especially when things *are* different now. After blindly walking through my life for so long, it feels like I've come alive again."

Frederick frowned. "Without me, you mean. You've come alive without me."

"It doesn't have anything to do with you," she said. He flinched, and she realized this wasn't coming out the way she'd hoped. "I mean, it does. This all has to do with you. You're the reason I had to reevaluate my entire life in the first place. But the funk, I fell into that on my own. And I had to get out of it on my own. I had to figure out what I wanted to do with the rest of my life. And now I have a career and friends. I like it here."

"I had no idea you felt so trapped in our life together," he said, bitterness creeping into his tone.

"I didn't feel trapped. But come on, Frederick, you weren't bored? There's no excuse for what you did, but don't you think, maybe, part of the reason you cheated was because you were looking for something new?"

"Annette, no—"

"It's okay if you were," Annette said. "It isn't my fault or your fault. It's life. But I don't know if I want to go back to that."

Frederick's shoulders sagged. "We can keep things interesting. We'll have a baby. You can't be bored with a baby. But even then, we can also go on more dates. Go out more. See more friends."

"It isn't just that." Annette pulled her hands free of his and folded them in front of her. "I'm not sure I want to be a stepmom."

"Wha—to Jackson? You don't want to..." He didn't seem capable of finishing his thought.

"I'm sorry," Annette said. "I really, really am. I feel awful. Because it isn't Jackson's fault. And you've apologized to me. I should be able to look past everything and love him, but I don't know if I want to."

"Annette—"

"I can forgive you, Frederick. I have already. But raising the child you had with another woman while you were cheating on me is..." She remembered what Natalie had said that morning. "It's a big ask. And I don't think I'm up for it."

She stayed quiet for a minute, until he took a step back from her. "That's it, then? You don't want to do it, so you aren't even going to try."

"It wouldn't be fair to you. Because I know how I feel."

"So my only option is to live here with you on the Isle of Palms and never see my son? That's not an option, Annie!"

"I know it's not," she said gently.

Frederick's face fell. He realized all at once what Annette was really saying. "You want a divorce."

The reality had hit her all at once that morning. The fact that she'd been more upset about leaving behind her family and her friends— Gregory, too—than the thought of leaving her husband meant something. And she couldn't ignore it.

"I'm sorry."

"You're sor—" he huffed. "That's what you say when you step on someone's foot. Not when you ask for a divorce."

"I am sorry, though. I should have done this a year ago. But—I don't know. I guess I wasn't ready to say goodbye then."

"But you are now?"

Annette nodded. "As ready as I'll ever be."

Frederick paced back and forth, his fists opening and closing at his sides. But Annette could see him losing steam as the situation set in. When he turned back to her, his face was smooth.

"We can work this out," he said. There wasn't any anger in his voice— or really any other emotion. Annette knew he didn't believe what he was saying. Not really.

"No, we can't. You're right; there isn't another option," she said. "You can't live here and never see your son."

"I'll get him on weekends. And for a month in the summer. I can visit him in Asheville, too."

"That's not what you want. And what do I do when Jackson visits you here?" she asked. "Should I go away for the weekend?"

"We'll figure something—"

"There isn't a compromise where children are involved. You have to be with someone who wants you *and* your son."

He looked down at her stomach. "And what about *our* child?"

Annette had imagined it a million times. When she and Frederick had a baby, they were supposed to weep with joy and fall into each other's arms. They were supposed to bicker about what color to paint the nursery and which car seat to buy. Frederick was supposed to lay his head on her stomach and talk to the baby every night.

But things changed. People changed. Annette didn't know what her future would look like, but for the first time since she'd found that lipstick print in Frederick's top drawer, she wasn't afraid.

"Now, *that* we will figure out. Together." She reached out and patted his elbow. "I promise."

18

AFTERNOON AT ISLE OF PALMS FARMERS MARKET

"Aunt Net! Look, Aunt Net! A tiger!"

Tyler had been dragging Annette around the Isle of Palms Farmer's Market for the better part of an hour. It was impressive how much stamina he had for a four-year-old.

But now, he was transfixed by a face painting station. The booth was set up under a large white tent with tacked-up pictures of kids painted to look like lions, tigers, and... well, no bears, but there were turtles. Annette was transfixed by the allure of shade.

"Do you want your face painted?" Annette hoped so. It would guarantee at least ten minutes of sitting down. Her feet were killing her.

"Ummmmm..."

"That little boy is turning into a shark," she said, pointing to a squirmy two-year-old. The painted teeth around his mouth were smudged because he kept leaning over to dip his finger in the paints.

"Ummmmm..."

"While you get your face painted, I'll buy you a donut from the bakery truck." Charlene didn't like when Annette bribed him, but desperate times called for deep-fried measures.

Unfortunately, the bribery worked too well.

"Donuts!" Tyler grabbed her hand and dragged Annette away from the blessed shade and towards the line for donuts.

That's where Charlene found them a few minutes later, still waiting in line. She walked over carrying a fresh bouquet of flowers and a clear plastic cup of iced tea. "I thought you were going to do face painting?"

"He wanted a donut instead."

"Aunt Net said I could—that she'd give me a donut if I got turned into a shark. But I don't want to be a shark. I just want a donut."

Charlene turned to Annette, eyebrow raised. "Aha, the bribery backfired?"

"I've learned my lesson."

"No, you haven't," Charlene laughed.

It was true. Annette was already formulating a bribery back-up plan for how she could convince Tyler to sit along the curb in the shade while they ate. Annette needed a break.

But she didn't get one for another hour. Tyler found an arts and crafts booth that was making bird feeders out of milk jugs. Then he found a penny candy stand and spent fifteen minutes pointing to every single bin of candy and asking for a detailed description of what it was, what it tasted like, and whether or not it would stick to his teeth.

"He's thorough," the old man running the booth said with a laugh. "Most kids dive in with both hands."

After they paid for their candy, Annette patted Tyler's sweaty head. "I think it's time for us to head home. It's hot out here, don't you think?"

Tyler panted dramatically, like he'd only just realized.

"Exactly," Annette smiled. "Do you have everything you wanted, Charlene?"

Her sister looked down at her bags of peaches and nectarines, fresh-cut bouquets, and the notecard-sized art print she'd bought to add to the gallery wall she'd been perfecting in the entryway. She nodded. "I hope so. And if not, that's fine. I wouldn't be able to carry it, anyway."

"Great. Then let's cut across the parking lot and get back to the car before I melt."

Before she could even finish her sentence, she saw it: a brunette woman pushing a rainbow-colored cart across the parking lot. A train of small children trailed behind her.

"Oh no."

The woman parked the cart, opened the cabinets on the side, and pulled out—

"Puppets!" Tyler shrieked. The woman pulled out two felt puppets and propped them on her knees. "I want to see the puppets. Can I see the puppets? Please!"

Annette knew there was no sense arguing. This battle was lost before it had even begun. "Fine," she sighed. "But after this, we are—"

Tyler didn't hear the rest of the sentence. He ran over to the group of kids and sat down in the middle of them, criss-cross-applesauce, ready for story time.

Charlene laughed and patted her back. "You're a good aunt."

"Who hosts a kids' story time in the smack dab middle of an asphalt parking lot in high summer?"

"It's the end of September," Charlene said. "And it's not miserably hot. You're just pregnant."

"The baby is the size of a blueberry. I don't think that's why I'm hot."

"No, it is," Charlene said. "It's been a long time, but I remember something about blood. You have more of it or less of it... I don't remember. But it's an internal thing and it makes you run warmer than normal."

Annette sighed. "Great. Yet another thing to look forward to. Any chance you're looking to move up north? Alaska, maybe?"

Charlene wrinkled her nose. "Prices would be ridiculous. Imagine how much diapers must cost there."

"Diapers. I forgot about diapers."

"And wipes," Charlene said. "And formula, if you end up going that route."

"I'll need to buy clothes."

"A lot of clothes. They grow so fast." Charlene began ticking things off on her fingers. "A bassinet, a crib, a changing table, a bouncy seat, burp cloths, teething toys—"

Suddenly, Annette could feel all of the extra blood in her body. It was all pumping through her heart, making each pulse feel like a bass drum in her chest.

Charlene was still going. "... pacifiers, a stroller, a car seat..."

Numbers and dollar signs flew at Annette like a swarm of bees. "Okay, I get it!"

"Oh, Annette, I'm—" Charlene wrapped an arm around her waist. "I'm sorry. I'll help you with everything, of course. All of Margaret's baby stuff is long gone, but I'm going to spoil my niece or nephew rotten. Just you wait."

Annette took a deep breath. "I know. But I don't want you to have to help. I want to do this on my own."

"You can't do everything on your own. And even if I didn't help, Frederick would. Wouldn't he?"

"I don't… Probably, yeah," she admitted. "Things are tense right now. After the divorce conversation, he kind of disappeared. But I'm sure he'll come around."

"He didn't take it well?"

"Would you?" Annette deadpanned. "He was shocked. And he had every right to be. I kept my feelings close to the chest the last few weeks."

"Just like you had every right to do," Charlene said. "He's the one who broke your trust to begin with."

"I know, but I feel like I led him on a bit. Actually, I feel like I've done that with a few different people."

Charlene shook her head. "You don't have anything to feel bad about. It's natural that you didn't fully trust Frederick with your every thought and feeling. He lost that privilege."

Annette chuckled darkly. "And what a privilege it is, being privy to all of my worries and random thoughts. Surely the line for people dying to know what I'm thinking must be miles long."

"It is a privilege," Charlene argued. "One that Gregory is happy to have, too. According to what you told me about your chat with him the other day, he was never upset with you about anything."

"That's because he is nice to a fault. He should be—"

"But he isn't. So let it go." Charlene floated a hand through the air, releasing invisible worries into the wind. "You have enough to worry about without making things up."

"Like how I'm going to afford a crib, a bassinet, a car seat, three different kinds of baby seats, towels for them to throw up on—"

"Exactly," Charlene laughed. "Worry about that and the rest will figure itself out."

Annette took a deep breath and tried to absorb what her sister was saying. It was too nice of a day to ruin it worrying about the future.

It was still ridiculously hot, yes, but a breeze had picked up. The palmetto trees that ringed the parking lot rustled. Laughter and conversation hummed in the background, not quite drowning out the june bugs and bird calls. The island felt like a dream sometimes, if only Annette took a moment to stop and breathe and listen.

Tyler was sitting stock still in the group of children, riveted by the woman's puppet show. Charlene kept picking up the bouquet from her bag and pressing it to her nose, literally stopping to smell the flowers. And Annette was grateful for all of it. For her family. The life she'd found here.

Without warning, she wrapped her arms around Charlene. "I love you."

"Oh, hello." Charlene laughed. "I love you, too."

"I'm glad I'm here."

Her sister raised a brow. "You really changed your tune from thirty seconds ago. I thought you wanted to leave."

"Not the farmer's market. Here, on the island. With you."

"Oh. Well, I'm glad you're here, too."

"This place has become my home," Annette said. "For right now, I'm not going to worry about the future. I'll probably freak out about it again later. But I'm content."

Charlene smiled. "That's amazing. But I don't think you have any reason to freak out."

"How could you possibly say that? My life is a mess."

"No, it's not!" Charlene said. "Annette, do you have any idea what you've accomplished this last year?"

"What? Getting divorced, moving in with my sister, taking a job with worse benefits than—"

Charlene set down her bags and grabbed Annette by the shoulders. "You started over. Completely. After fifteen years of marriage, you picked up, moved out, and started over. That's incredible."

Annette's face grew warm. "It's not that impressive."

"Listen, I don't want to slap a pregnant woman, least of all my sister. But I'll do it if you make me," Charlene warned. "Because I am so incredibly proud of you. You did the scary thing, Annette. You started over when most people would have been frozen in fear. It's amazing."

Tears burned at the back of Annette's eyes, and she blinked them back. She did not want to cry in front of a crowd of strangers and two very strange looking felt puppets.

"You have big things on the horizon, but there is no doubt in my mind that you'll figure it all out."

She swallowed down a lump in her throat. "You really think so?"

"I know so," Charlene said confidently. "I'm so proud of who you are. Only good things are ahead."

A tear rolled down her cheek, and she reached up to swipe it away. "I'm going to be a single mom."

Charlene nodded and pulled Annette in for a hug. "That's true. But you'll never be alone."

19

THAT NIGHT AT ANNETTE'S HOUSE

Annette meant what she'd said earlier: she wasn't going to worry about the future. But not worrying didn't mean she couldn't plan.

"Do you remember everything Aunt Charlene said I needed for you?" She gave her stomach a small poke. "A crib and a bassinet—why do I need both? What's the difference?"

She grabbed her pen and wrote both items down on the growing list she'd started in the back of her planner. The baby would arrive in May, which felt far away, but Annette knew the next nine months would fly by.

After making the additions, she tossed her planner on the nightstand and flopped back in bed. Her entire body hurt. Walking around the farmer's market and then taking Tyler to the park, where he'd insisted Aunt Net had to go down every slide with him, would have been exhausting on any normal day. But now she was in her first trimester and dealing with full-force nausea and exhaustion.

"For someone so small, you're causing a big fuss," she whispered. "And I doubt I'll get much of a break once you're here, either. I hear newborns are pretty demanding."

Still, Annette smiled at the thought. "You'll be worth it, though. I can tell."

How long had she spent dreaming of holding her baby in her arms? For years, she'd prayed for a missed period. Then she'd swallowed down her disappointment when life kept going right on schedule. Eventually, she'd stopped expecting anything at all.

And now she was going to be a mom.

"I guess I'm already a mom," she mumbled. "Technically."

Technicality or not, she'd take it. She was going to be in charge of caring for a walking, talking, living human being. And now that her life was beginning to settle somewhat, she could finally focus on the supernova-sized bright spot that had come out of all of the chaos: this new, precious life.

Then her phone rang. *Speaking of the chaos.*

"Hey, Freddie." Annette did her best to sound friendly and neutral, even though she had no idea where he was on the path to acceptance. Denial? Anger?

"Hey, Annie. How are you?"

He sounded normal as far as Annette could tell, but it wasn't much to go on. She couldn't relax just yet.

"I'm fine. How are you?"

"I've been better," he sighed. "But I've been worse, too. How are you?"

"You already asked me that."

"Oh. I meant, like, how are you feeling? Are you having any symptoms?"

"Nausea. Lots and lots of nausea," she said. "I'm basically sucking on ginger candies all day long."

"I'm sorry," he said. "My sister told me to suggest you wear sea sickness bands."

"You told Amber?"

He winced. "Sorry. I know I wasn't supposed to tell, but... well, I needed to talk to someone. About the baby. About everything, really."

"I get it. I told Charlene. I can't really begrudge you Amber."

They fell into a long silence that Annette finally broke.

"Did you need something?"

"Yeah, sorry. I called to—to talk to you. Obviously." He chuckled anxiously. "But I'm not doing a great job of it."

"You're doing fine."

"It's just you. I've been talking to you on the phone for fifteen years. Longer, actually," he said. "We used to sit on the phone for hours in college. Remember that?"

Annette felt a pang in her chest. "Yeah, I do."

"That was never awkward. We always had something to say. But... I think there's something to what you said on the beach the other day. About the quiet in our house." He paused and took a breath. "We kind of ran out of things to say, didn't we?"

"It happens," she said softly. "We wouldn't be the first to... fall out of love."

She heard his sharp intake of breath. "Maybe not. But it's the first time for us. And it hurts."

There was no slow build-up to the tears this time. Nothing for Annette to blink back and fight against. The onslaught was sudden and serious. Tears poured down her cheeks before she knew what was happening.

"I know it was my decision, but it hurts me, too."

"I know." His voice was gentle. "I know you didn't do this to hurt me. Or punish me. That's not who you are."

"I really have forgiven you. For everything. I hope you know that."

"I know you have. Now, we just have to see if I can forgive myself."

"I hope you can." Annette sniffled.

"Uh-oh," he said. "Are you crying? Did I make you cry? That isn't why I called."

"Making me cry isn't exactly a feat these days. I cried at a dog food commercial this morning."

"Darn hormones."

"'*Darn them to heck,*' as your mother used to say."

Frederick laughed. "She always loved you. At the end, I think she preferred you to me."

"She did not!"

"She did," he said. "But who could blame her? The day we got married, she told me you were a 'one-in-a-million woman.' And she wasn't wrong. You're special, Annie. I'm sorry I messed everything up."

"It wasn't all you, Frederick. I had my role in things, too."

"You didn't. But thanks for saying so." He sighed again. "Well, I guess I'll get to it. I called to say—I want you to know I'll do whatever you want. I've made things hard enough. The last year—the last few years, really—has been tough for you. So I don't want to fight you on anything."

"You're talking about the divorce?"

"I hate that word. *Divorce.* It sounds so depressing. I never thought I'd be getting divorced."

"Me neither," she said. "Even when things were hard—with infertility. And the times where it felt like we weren't connecting. I always thought we'd work through them. I never imagined a life without you. I didn't plan for this."

"Which is why I'll sign whatever you want and agree to whatever you want," he said. "I don't want to drag this process out any more than necessary. I want you to be able to focus on your health and our baby's health. And I'll do whatever I can to make things easier for you. Knowing you, you'll want to do everything yourself."

"Have you been talking to Charlene?" she teased.

"I don't need to. I know you well enough," he said. "You'll want to do it all solo, but please let me help. Tell me what you need, and I'll make sure you have it. I don't want you to stress about anything."

"Thank you, Frederick."

"It's the least I can do," he said. "And when I figure out where I'll be— whether I'm going back to Asheville or somewhere in the middle—we can set custody terms. But I really don't want to fight with you."

"I don't, either. I just want what's fair."

"I don't."

Annette frowned. "What? You don't want things to be fair?"

"If I got what was fair, I'd never see you or our baby again," he said. "I want grace. Lots and lots of grace."

Annette didn't like hearing Frederick be so down on himself. But she could understand it. He was hurting, and nothing either of them could say would change the fact that it was his fault. If he hadn't cheated, they'd probably still be married. They likely wouldn't be having this conversation at all.

"Things happen how they're supposed to," she said finally. "For some reason, this is how we were meant to end up. And I hope you'll make your peace with it eventually."

"I hope so, too," he said. "And I also hope that, maybe, somehow… maybe we could be friends someday? That seems ridiculous to say. We've been married or dating for two decades. How could we go back to being just friends? But… I'd rather be your friend than nothing at all."

Realizing it would be harder for her to say goodbye to her sister and her friends in IOP than Frederick had made Annette's decision for her. But that didn't mean it wouldn't be hard to say goodbye to him. It didn't mean she didn't want Frederick in her life at all. Drama and mistakes aside, they'd lived a lot of life together. And Annette didn't want to let all of that go.

She'd been a lot of things to Frederick. She'd been his girlfriend and his fiancé; she'd been his wife and a scorned woman. Now, she was the mother of his baby. But maybe, after all the ups and downs, it was time for a new title.

"Do you think we can be friends?" he asked again, tentative.

Annette smiled. "After everything we've been through, I'm sure we can manage that."

20

A WEEK LATER AT GREGORY DANE'S HOUSE

Annette scooped a handful of flour out of the canister and sprinkled it across Gregory's countertop. "Sorry again for destroying your kitchen. Charlene has barred me from using ours for the foreseeable future."

"You can't use your own kitchen? That doesn't seem fair."

"Apparently, it took her a full two days to clean up after my last baking binge. She's still a little bitter."

"Oh." Gregory stepped back and took a long look at their workspace. "Well, she isn't wrong. You're kind of a messy cook."

"True art cannot be contained."

He snorted. "Does true art also use someone else's recipe?"

Annette huffed and began rolling out the dough a little more aggressively. "Listen, buster, do you want my help or not?"

"Of course I do. I'm the one who had to schedule this lesson, remember? I couldn't let you back out of our deal."

"I wasn't going to back out! I'm just a very busy woman."

A bit too busy throwing up, that is.

Morning sickness had hit Annette especially hard the last few days. She'd had to video call into a few speech therapy sessions. On more than one occasion, she'd dipped off screen to get sick while a student looked on, horrified. It wasn't pretty.

"I'm just glad you could make room for me in your very busy schedule," he teased. "I've been looking forward to it."

"Me too."

And she meant it. Even though Gregory had been the one to reach out first after their lunch on the beach, Annette had been trying to work up the courage for days.

It was just that, when she'd last talked with Gregory, she and Frederick were planning to stay together. They were going to stay married and raise their child together. And that meant she and Gregory would be friends. But now...

Well, now, everything had changed—yet again. She was getting a divorce and planning to be a single mother. She was staying on the Isle of Palms. It was the second time her life had done an abrupt about-face in only a matter of days. And Annette wasn't sure how to broach the subject with Gregory without sounding like her life was some kind of reality television special.

"Okay." Gregory clapped his hands. "So far, we've just made pastry dough. And while it looks great, I know how to do that part."

"If you want to speed up the process, make yourself useful and get me a pastry cutter and a pie dish."

He clicked his heels together and offered a crisp salute. "Ma'am, yes, ma'am." Gregory banged around the kitchen for a minute and returned with the necessary tools. "Your tools, Doctor. Now show me your soggy bottom secrets."

Annette laughed. "Okay. I assume you're already blind baking your crusts?"

"Yes," he nodded. "I put the crust in for about ten minutes before I add my fillings."

"Do you do anything else before adding your fillings?"

He narrowed his eyes at her. "Is this a trick question?"

"No," she laughed. "Just a normal question."

"Okay. Then no. I don't do anything else."

"Oh boy."

"What?"

Annette shook her head. "This isn't good."

His eyes widened. "What? What's not good? What's happening?"

"I hope you didn't have plans. Because we're going to be here for a while." Annette smiled. "Do you have more pie dishes?"

In the end, they made four different quiches, each one trying a slightly different method. On one, they did a simple blind bake. On the next, they brushed the blind-baked crust with an egg white wash to help protect it from the fillings. On the third, they pre-cooked the vegetables and the sausage to reduce how much moisture would be released during baking. And on the fourth and final quiche, they did all the tricks.

By the time everything was said and done, they had four full-sized quiches cooling on the counter and a disaster zone of a kitchen to clean.

Gregory leaned on the island, his elbow resting in a pile of flour, and wiped his brow. "I run a restaurant. How is it I'm tired after making four quiches?"

"Because I can be hard to keep up with," she teased. "But really, these days just waking up makes me tired."

"How are you doing with all that? The pregnancy, I mean. Aside from being tired?"

"Oh, I'm fine." Annette waved him away. "Morning sickness and cravings. Nothing too serious."

Not physically, at least. But Annette didn't want to dump her drama on him. Especially since she didn't know if it would change things between them. Or—maybe worse—if it wouldn't change anything at all.

"And how's Frederick?" Gregory sounded normal enough, but he glanced at the floor as he asked. His fingers nervously doodled in the leftover sprinkled flour across the countertop.

"He's, um, fine," she shrugged. "I'm guessing. I don't know. I haven't really seen him."

"You haven't seen him?"

"Not since he went back to Asheville." Annette was being weird, she knew she was being weird, she could hear herself being weird... but she couldn't seem to stop.

Gregory frowned. "Did he go back for a quick trip, or...?"

"Permanently, I think." Annette swallowed. "Since we decided to split up, he didn't really need to be here."

Gregory looked up at her, but didn't say anything.

"We decided to get divorced," she blurted finally. "I asked him for a divorce. Last week. We are getting a divorce."

Now that she'd said the word, she couldn't seem to stop saying it. *Divorcedivorcedivorce.* Annette barely resisted the urge to clap a hand over her mouth, or to dive face-first into one of the still-hot quiches.

"Oh." Gregory nodded slowly. "Okay. Wow."

"Yeah."

"Was I supposed to see that coming?" he asked.

"Frederick sure didn't." At that, Annette did at last clap a hand on her mouth. "Oh my goodness, that sounded horrible. I just mean... No. No, you shouldn't have seen it coming. I barely saw it coming."

"Okay." He nodded slowly again. "So, divorce. You're getting divorced."

"I am."

The kitchen was still toasty from the hours the oven had been on, but Annette was sweltering. She needed to crack a window open.

"I'm sorry, I should have led with 'I'm sorry.'" He shook his head. "I mean... sorry I didn't say sorry sooner. That's the normal thing to say in this situation."

Annette laughed softly. "Believe me, I'm no judge of normal right now."

"Was it because of me?"

Annette inhaled sharply. "Was what?"

"That was another weird thing to say," he said with a wince. "I'm sorry. But... the divorce. Did you get divorced because of me? Carly Simon should write a song about me. '*I'm so vain, I probably think this divorce is about me.*'"

Annette had never seen Gregory so out of sorts. She felt bad for causing it, but it was nice to know she wasn't the only one feeling frazzled.

"It's not vain. I've thought about it, too," she whispered.

And she had, many times. It was impossible not to wonder whether Gregory had something to do with her decision to divorce Frederick.

A lot of neutral observers would certainly think so. A handsome restaurant owner comes into her life and teaches her to make delicious scones, and suddenly she is getting a divorce? Put two and two together, you know? She could understand that line of thinking. But the truth was, as always seemed to be the case with her, far more complicated.

"Honestly, no," she said. "You weren't the reason. You helped me decide, but I'm not getting divorced because of you."

He sighed. "Good. Maybe some people would be flattered, but I would have felt horrible."

"Because you're a nice guy," she said softly. "That's part of the reason why you helped me decide. You and Charlene and everyone else here I love—I'd hate to leave any of you behind. More than I'd hate being without Frederick."

"So, if he'd agreed to stay on the island … you would have stayed together?"

Annette shook her head. "No. I mean, maybe we would have made it work for a while. But our issues were bigger than that. He broke my trust, and even though I've forgiven him, some things can't be repaired. We always would have ended up this way, I think."

There was a long stretch of silence, but it didn't feel fraught. Annette felt comfortable giving Gregory time to absorb what this meant. For the first time in a long time, she felt at ease.

Finally, he took a deep breath. "Can I be honest?"

"That depends. Have you been lying so far?"

He smiled but didn't laugh. "No, but what I'm about to say is really honest. So I want to prepare you."

Annette stood up tall and pretended to brace herself. "I'm prepared."

"I like you, Annette."

Annette suspected this already. But her heart still fluttered.

"I like you quite a bit," he continued. "And I'm glad you didn't get a divorce because of me. But I'd be lying if I said I didn't hope this divorce might benefit me in some way."

"And you can't lie. Because we're being honest right now," she said.

"Yes," he chuckled. "I'm being very, very, embarrassingly honest."

"If it helps with the embarrassment, I like you, too," she murmured.

He grinned. "That does help. Quite a bit, actually. Thank you."

"You're welcome." Annette tried to keep her face serious, but her mouth kept tipping up at the corners.

Gregory shoved his wavy red hair away from his forehead. "I know you've got a lot going on right now. Way too much for me to be burdening you with this at all, but… well, if the time was ever right and you were interested then, I'd like to be more than friends with you."

Annette's heart was full on flying now. If she wasn't careful, she thought it might propel straight through her chest. "Okay."

"I'm happy to be friends with you. I'd rather that than nothing—but, yeah. More than friends would be great, too." He shook his head. "I feel like a middle school boy asking you to the dance. Are you getting that vibe, too?"

"Maybe just a little bit," she admitted with a smile. "But it's sweet.' Thank you."

He smiled up at her, and Annette held it for a second. Letting the moment resonate. Making sure, even though she didn't say it out loud, that Gregory Dane understood how she felt.

Then the moment passed and they looked away.

"Next question," he said. "What are we going to do with four quiches?"

Annette grinned mischievously. "I have an idea."

21

THAT NIGHT AT ANNETTE'S HOUSE

"You do know I have a catering fee, right?" Gregory asked as he brought the last two quiches into her kitchen. "I feel like I've been bamboozled."

"Bamboozled," Tyler repeated. He rolled the word clumsily around his mouth, testing it. "Bam-BOO-zled. What's that?"

"It means I've been tricked. Conned. Hoodwinked. It means your Aunt Net is a swindler." Gregory slid the quiches onto the island. "I had no idea I was cooking for a party."

"As soon as we cut into these bad boys and you taste how delicious and not soggy the crust is, you'll realize I've already paid you," Annette said confidently. "Actually, you'll realize my tips are priceless. Front Beachtro is going to be known the world over for having the least soggy pastry bottoms in existence."

Gregory rolled his eyes, but couldn't keep from smiling. "Who all is coming to this party, anyway?"

"It's just a few friends," Annette said. "My sister and Noah, our neighbor Elaine, my friend from work, Natalie. Me. Tyler. And now you, obviously."

"Glad to be included amongst your friends." He winked, and Annette felt the curious thud of her heart she was beginning to associate with Gregory.

Really, Annette *had* swindled Gregory. Just a little. Charlene had planned a small party in Annette's honor, and she'd planned all along to serve the quiches they made for dinner. But what the man didn't know wouldn't hurt him.

"This way you can announce your pregnancy to all your friends at once," Charlene had said. "It will be a nice time."

The thought was nice, but Annette knew her sister better than that. Really, Charlene just wanted to make sure Annette knew she had support. That, even though she and Frederick weren't together, she had people to depend on. As much as Annette didn't like making a fuss or asking for help and as cheesy as the idea seemed, she could do with the reminder that she wasn't in it alone.

"Everyone will be here in the next couple minutes," she said. "I'll start slicing the quiche, and you start chopping the garnish."

"I'm a guest. Should I really be chopping my own garnish?"

Annette pressed a bunch of chives against his chest. "I may be the pastry expert, but you're the chef. Start chopping."

"Ma'am, yes, ma'am."

Fifteen minutes later, they were sitting around a long folding table with all of Annette's friends, eating delicious quiche.

"Okay," Natalie said, raising her fork in the air. "All of the quiches are good, but the one at the end here is the best. The crust is perfect."

"Which number is that?" Annette asked.

Charlene read the note card taped to the side of the pie dish. "Number four."

"Another vote for number four," Gregory said. "That settles it. The 'all of the above' pastry wins."

"It's more work to blind bake and do an egg wash and pre-cook your meat and veggies, but you can't argue with the results," Annette agreed.

"I don't like any of them," Tyler announced. "They're yucky."

Charlene gave Gregory an apologetic smile and patted Tyler's head. "You didn't even try one, bud. You ate a peanut butter and jelly sandwich."

"Because those are yucky." He wrinkled his nose.

Noah laughed. "Sorry, Chef Gregory, but I don't think Front Beachtro is going to crack the four-year-old demographic anytime soon."

"It is what it is," Gregory shrugged. "Maybe I'll work on updating my kids' menu. Any thoughts, Tyler? What's your favorite food?"

"Crunchy tacos!" he said, bouncing up and down in his chair.

"Crunchy tacos without lettuce or tomatoes or sour cream. And no beans. And just a dash of seasoning," Charlene amended. "All important notes."

Gregory pretended to take notes. "Okay. Unseasoned ground beef with cheese in a crunchy shell. I think it'll be a hit."

While everyone talked, Annette couldn't wipe the smile off of her face. Gregory fit in with her family and friends so easily, like he'd always been there.

Elaine leaned forward. "I'll have to pay you to make these for me, Gregory."

"For friends, I cook for free," he demurred.

Annette lightly slapped his shoulder. "That's not what you said in the kitchen, Mr. I-Have-A-Catering-Fee."

"I'd pay you," Elaine insisted. "It would be for business."

"What business?" Charlene asked.

Elaine smiled and sat up straighter. "Well, I have sort of an announcement, actually."

"Uh-oh," Charlene laughed. "We're all ears."

Tyler gave Elaine a little drumroll with his fork and knife on the table, and then Elaine took a deep breath and said, "Instead of selling my home… I've decided to turn it into a boarding house of sorts. A bed and breakfast, you might call it. And I'd love to have these quiches for breakfasts for the guests."

"I love that idea!" Annette crowed at once. "Are you taking reservations? Put me down as the first guest!"

"You'll all be invited to the soft opening. Free of charge, of course. I'll want all of your feedback and comments," Elaine said.

"I'd never turn down a free staycation," Natalie said.

Annette nodded. "Agreed. But I'll pay double. I want to be a paying customer."

"She has never once said that to me," Gregory joked. "Count yourself lucky, Elaine."

Annette elbowed Gregory in the ribs while everyone laughed.

Once everyone was finished eating, Charlene stood up at the end of the table. For a second, it looked like she was going to tap her plastic fork against the side of her plastic cup to get everyone's attention. But in the end, she just cleared her throat.

"Hey, everyone. Thanks for coming tonight. I know it was short notice. But I wanted to get all of the people who love Annette together in one place."

Everyone looked at Annette. She felt her face flush hot.

Charlene continued, "Annette is as stubborn as she is independent. Which can be a dangerous combination."

"I object," Annette said.

"What's new?" Charlene rolled her eyes and kept going. "Annette has been through so much in the last year, and she has handled it all with grace and dignity. But on this next adventure, I want to make sure she has all the support she'll need."

"What adventure?" Natalie asked, looking around the table. Her eyes landed on Annette. "Are you leaving? I thought you'd decided to stay!"

"I am staying," Annette reassured her. "I'm not going anywhere. But… I'm pregnant."

Natalie gasped. "No, you're not! Really?"

"Really," Annette laughed.

Her friend jumped up and ran over to give her a hug. "Congratulations! This is amazing news. I'm so happy for—" She looked around the table. Everyone else was smiling pleasantly. "Why am I the only one freaking out?"

"I think you might have been the only one who didn't know," Annette whispered.

Charlene frowned. "Is that true? Did everyone else—" Her shoulders sagged. "I was making this a big announcement, but everyone already knew?"

"Frederick told me," Gregory said.

Noah nodded. "You told me, Char. And Tyler found out when you told me. Little eavesdropper."

"I'm going to have a cousin!" Tyler grinned.

"I think I was the first one to find out, as a matter of fact," Elaine chuckled. "Annette came to my house after she got done at the doctor's office."

Natalie tugged playfully on Annette's hair. "I'll try not to take it personally that you didn't tell me."

"Believe me, it wasn't personal," Annette assured her. "I had no idea there were so many loose lips in this group. Any ships in the vicinity are in danger."

"Well, this is amazing," Natalie said firmly. "And whatever you need, I'm here for you."

"Me, too!" Elaine agreed.

"And obviously, Tyler, Noah, and I are here for you, too."

Gregory leaned over, voice low. "And don't forget about me, Annette. Whatever you need... I'm yours."

Late That Night At The Beach

"Tyler lets Noah read books to him now?" Annette asked. "That's a development."

After cleaning up the kitchen, she and Charlene had decided to walk off the quiche down at the beach. Noah stayed behind to put Tyler to bed.

"A hard-won development," Charlene said, kicking at the sand with her bare foot. "Noah has been trying to convince him for months. I'm glad they worked it out. It's nice to have a break from bedtime duty occasionally."

"Absence makes the heart grow fonder. Have you told Tyler that?"

Charlene laughed. "He's more of a *'Never leaving each other's side and doing everything together makes the heart grow fonder'* kind of kid."

"I guess I can't blame him for that."

"After everything he's been through?" Charlene shook her head. "After his mom abandoning him so suddenly, his therapist said it's normal for him to have attachment issues. It's just something we'll have to work on."

"And now that I'm not moving back to Asheville, that's one less thing to worry about."

Charlene nodded, but it was stiff. Her lips were pressed together so tight they practically glowed white in the darkness.

"What?" Annette asked. "Why do you look like that?"

"Nothing," Charlene said. "It isn't important."

Annette stopped walking. "What is it, Char?"

"I don't want to get into it. Not tonight. Tonight is supposed to be about you."

"It was about me. But everyone is gone now, so this can be about you." She stepped closer, fear sending a shiver down her spine. "What's up?"

Charlene sighed. "I didn't want to do this today. Because I'm going to be there to support you no matter what. And I don't want you to worry about anything."

"Okay. But you're officially worrying me right now," she said. "What is it? Are... are you sick?"

The thought felt like plunging into an ice bath. It crushed her. She'd lived without her sister for five years, and she never wanted to go back to that. Ever. She couldn't handle it if she—

"No." Charlene reached for Annette's hand and squeezed. "I'm fine. It's not that. It's good news, actually. At least, I think it is."

Annette sighed. "I'll be angry with you for scaring me to death later. But for now, for the love of God, please tell me the good news."

Charlene took a deep breath. "Noah and I talked recently, and… we've decided maybe the time has come for him to—for us to live together." She tried to suppress her smile but failed. It spread across her face like a sunrise, slowly at first and then faster and faster until she glowed with it. "He's going to move in with me."

"Charlene!" Annette hugged her sister. "Congratulations! I'm so happy for you."

"Thanks. Thank you. I know we've moved kind of fast, but—"

"When you know, you know," Annette said. "I think it's wonderful."

"Me too. I couldn't be happier, but—"

"But what?"

"Well, he's going to sell his house. And once that happens, he'll move in with me," Charlene said slowly. "And we've talked about it, and we don't expect you to move out right away. You have a lot going on right now. With the baby and everything. But eventually, you know, we'll want… we'll want our own space." Charlene slapped a hand on her forehead. "I feel awful. You're pregnant, and I'm kicking you out. I'm the worst. I'm so sorry."

Annette shook Charlene by the shoulders. "Hey. You are not the worst. You're moving on with your life and it's amazing. I'm so happy for you."

"But what about you?" Charlene asked.

"I'll figure it out." Annette waved her sister off. "Someone recently told me that no matter what comes my way, I'll be able to figure it out. So that's what I'll do."

"Which incredibly smart person could have told you that?"

Annette shrugged. "Some jerk who is kicking me out of her house."

"Hey!"

"I'm kidding," Annette said. "Really, I'll be fine. It's not going to be the easiest thing, but since when has life ever been easy?"

Charlene sighed. "True."

Annette looked out over the ocean. The dark blue waves rose up to the moonlight and crashed back down into the surf. Her life had been a lot like the ocean. An endless series of high points and low points. But one thing remained true: she always found her way back to the surface.

She wrapped an arm around her sister and pulled her in close. "I have no idea what comes next for me. But for the first time in a while, I'm really excited to find out."

Check out THE BEACH B&B, Book 3 in the Sunny Isle of Palms series, to find out what happens next!
The Beach B&B

SNEAK PREVIEW OF NO HOME LIKE NANTUCKET

If you loved **The Beach Baby**, *you'll fall head over heels for the Benson family in my beloved Sweet Island Inn series, set on the gorgeous island of Nantucket.*

Take a sneak preview below of Book 1 in the series, NO HOME LIKE NANTUCKET.

≈

NO HOME LIKE NANTUCKET:
A Sweet Island Inn Novel (Book 1)

Nantucket was their paradise—until reality came barging in.

An unexpected pregnancy.

A marriage on the rocks.

A forbidden workplace romance.

And a tragedy no one could have seen coming.

Take a trip to Nantucket's Sweet Island Inn and follow along as Mae Benson and her children—the Wall Street queen Eliza, stay-at-home mom Holly, headstrong chef Sara, and happy-go-lucky fisherman Brent—face the hardest summer of their lives.

Love, loss, heartbreak, hope—it's all here and more. Can the Benson family find a way to forgive themselves and each other? Or will their grief be too much to overcome?

Find out in **NO HOME LIKE NANTUCKET.**

Click here to start reading now!

~

Chapter One: Mae

Mae Benson never ever slept in.

For each of the one thousand, two hundred, and eleven days that she'd lived at 114 Howard Street, Nantucket, Massachusetts, she'd gotten up with the dawn and started her morning the second her eyes opened. It wasn't because she was a busybody, or compulsive, or obsessive. On the contrary, snoozing for a while was tempting. Her bed was soft this morning. The first fingers of springtime sunlight had barely begun to peek in through the gauzy curtains that hung over the window. And she was in that perfect sleeping position—warm but not too warm, wrapped up but not too tightly.

But force of habit could sometimes be awfully hard to break. So, being careful to make as little noise as possible, she slid out from underneath the comforter, tucked her feet into the fuzzy slippers she'd received for her sixtieth birthday last year, and rose.

Her husband, Henry, always called her his little hummingbird. He'd even bought her a beautiful handblown hummingbird ornament for Christmas last year from a glassblower down by the wharf. It had jade-green wings, little amethysts for eyes, and a patch of ruby red on its chest. She loved how it caught and refracted the winter sunbeams, and she always made sure to put it on a limb of the tree where it could see the snow falling outdoors.

"Flitting around the house, are we?" Henry would say, laughing, every time he came downstairs from their master bedroom to find Mae buzzing from corner to corner. She would just laugh and shake her head. He could make fun of her all he wanted, but the fact remained that each of the little projects she had running at all times around the house required love and care from the moment the day began.

She ran through the list in her head as she moved silently around the bedroom getting dressed for the day. She needed to water the plants on the living room windowsill, the ones that her daughter, Sara, had sent from her culinary trip to Africa and made her mother promise to keep alive until she could retrieve them on her next visit. Crane flowers, with their gorgeous mix of orange- and blue-bladed leaves; desert roses, with their soft blush of red fading into the purest white; and her favorites, the fire lilies, that looked just like a flickering flame.

She had to check on the batch of marshmallow fluff fudge—a Mae Benson specialty—that she'd left to set in the freezer overnight. Her friend Lola, who lived down the street, had just twisted her ankle badly a few days prior and was laid up at home with a boot on her leg. Mae didn't know much about ankle injuries, but she had a lot of hands-on experience with fudge, so she figured she'd offer what she knew best.

She should also start coffee for Henry—lots of cream and sugar, as always. Henry had an outing planned that morning with Brent to go check on some fishing spots they'd been scheming over for the last few weeks. Mae knew he was excited about the trip. He'd been exhibiting trademark Happy Henry behavior all week long—eyes lighting up with that mischievous twinkle, hands rubbing together like an evil mastermind, and the way that he licked the corner of his lips, like he could already taste the salt air that hung on the wind and feel the bouncing of the boat as it raced through the waves.

Just before she turned to leave the bedroom and start her day, she looked over at her husband. He was sleeping on his side of the bed, snoring softly like he always did. It was never enough to wake her, thankfully. Not like Lola's ex-husband, who'd been a snorer of epic proportions. Henry hadn't bothered a single soul in the six and a half decades he'd been alive on this earth. Matter of fact, she couldn't think of a single person who disliked him—other than Mae herself, whenever he took the liberty of dipping into the brownie batter, or when he insisted on sneaking up behind her while she was cooking, nipping at the lobe of her ear, then dancing away and laughing when she tried to swat him with a spoon and inevitably sprayed chocolate batter all over the kitchen.

But the truth of the matter was that she could never bring herself to stay irked at him. It wasn't just his physical looks, although he certainly wasn't hurting in that department. The same things she'd fallen in love with at that Boston bar forty-plus years ago were still present and accounted for. The long, proud nose. Full lips, always eager to twitch into a smile. Bright blue eyes that danced in the sunlight when he laughed, cried, and—well, all the time, really. And that darn shock of hair that was perpetually threatening to fall over his forehead. She reached over and smoothed it out of his face now. Time had turned his sun-drenched blondness into something more silvery, but in Mae's eyes, he was all the more handsome for it.

But, even more than his good looks, Mae loved Henry's soul. He was a selfless giver, an instant friend to every child who'd ever come across his path. He loved nothing more than to kneel in front of an awestruck five-year-old and present him or her with some little hand-carved trinket, one of the many he kept in his pockets to whittle whenever he had an idle moment. She loved that he laughed and cried in all the wrong places during romantic comedies and that he knew how to cook—how to *really* cook, the kind of cooking you do with a jazz record crooning through the speakers and a soft breeze drifting in through an open window.

She let her hand linger on Henry's forehead just a beat too long. He didn't open his eyes, but his hand snaked up from underneath the sheets and threaded through Mae's fingers.

"You're getting up?"

"Can't waste the day away."

It was a ritual, one they'd been through practically every morning for as long as either could remember. For all that he'd become a proud father to four children, a state-record-holding fisherman, a much-sought-after contractor and builder on the island of Nantucket, Henry loved nothing so much as to stay in bed for hours, alternating between sleeping and poking Mae until she rolled over and gave him the soft kisses he called her "hummingbird pecks." There was a perpetual little boy spirit in him, a playfulness that another six or sixty decades couldn't extinguish if it tried.

"Stay with me," he murmured. "The day can wait a few more minutes, can't it?" His eyes were open now, heavy with sleep, but still gazing at her fondly.

Mae tapped him playfully on the tip of the nose. "If it was up to you, 'a few more minutes' would turn into hours before we knew it, and then I'd be scrambling around like a chicken with my head cut off, trying to get everything done before Holly, Pete, and the kids get here tonight."

Holly was Mae and Henry's middle daughter. She and her husband, Pete, were bringing their two kids to Nantucket to spend the weekend. Mae had had the date circled on her calendar for months, excited at the prospect of spoiling her grandkids rotten. She already had oodles of activities planned—walks downtown to get rock candy from the corner store, sandcastles at the beach, bike rides down to 'Sconset to ogle the grand houses the rich folks had built out on that end of the island.

Grady was a little wrecking ball of a seven-year-old boy, and Mae knew that he'd love nothing so much as building a massive sandcastle and then terrorizing it like a blond Godzilla. Alice, on the other hand, was still as sweet and loving as a five-year-old girl could be. She let Grandma Mae braid her long, soft hair into fishtails every morning whenever they were visiting the island. It was another ritual that Mae treasured beyond anything else. Her life was full of those kinds of moments.

"It ain't so bad, lying in bed with me, is it?" Henry teased. "But maybe I just won't give ya a choice!"

He leaped up and threw his arms around Mae's waist, tugging her over him and then dragging them both beneath the covers. Mae yelped in surprise and smacked him on the chest, but Henry was a big man—nearly six and a half feet tall—and the years he'd spent hauling in fish during his weekend trips with Brent had kept him muscular and toned. When her palm landed on his shoulder, it just made a thwacking noise, and did about as much good as if she'd slapped a brick wall. So she just laughed and let Henry pull her into his arms, roll over on top of her, and throw the comforter over their heads.

It was soft and warm and white underneath. The April sun filtered through the bedsheets and cast everything in a beautiful, hazy glow. "You've never looked so beautiful," Henry said, his face suspended above hers.

"Henry Benson, I do believe you are yanking my chain," she admonished.

"Never," he said, and he said it with such utter seriousness that Mae's retort fell from her lips. Instead of poking him in the chest like she always did whenever he teased her, she let her hand stroke the line of his jaw.

He pressed a gentle kiss to her lips. "Stay with me for just a few more minutes, Mrs. Benson," he said. She could feel him smiling as he kissed her. She could also feel the butterflies fluttering in her stomach. Forty-one years of marriage and four children later, and she still got butterflies when her husband kissed her. Wasn't that something?

"All right, Mr. Benson," she said, letting her head fall back on the pillows. "Just a few more minutes."

Henry grinned and fell in next to her, pulling her into his embrace. She could feel his heartbeat thumping in his chest. Familiar. Dependent. Reliable. Hers. "You just made my day."

"But I'm warning you," she continued, raising one finger into the air and biting back the smile that wanted to steal over her lips. "If you start snoring again, I'm smothering you with a pillow."

"Warning received," Henry said. "Now quit making a fuss and snooze with me for a while, darling."

So Mae did exactly that. Sara's plants could wait.

Click here to keep reading!

JOIN MY MAILING LIST!

Click the link below to join my mailing list and receive updates, freebies, release announcements, and more!

JOIN HERE:

https://sendfox.com/lp/19y8p3

ALSO BY GRACE PALMER

Sunny Isle of Palms

The Beach Baby

The Beach Date

The Beach B&B

The Wayfarer Inn

The Vineyard Sisters

The Vineyard Mothers

The Vineyard Daughters

Sweet Island Inn

No Home Like Nantucket (Book 1)

No Beach Like Nantucket (Book 2)

No Wedding Like Nantucket (Book 3)

No Love Like Nantucket (Book 4)

No Secret Like Nantucket (Book 5)

No Forever Like Nantucket (Book 6)

Willow Beach Inn

Just South of Paradise (Book 1)

Just South of Perfect (Book 2)

Just South of Sunrise (Book 3)

Just South of Christmas (Book 4)